Gothic

Andrew Taylor is the author of a number of crime novels, including the ground-breaking Roth Trilogy, which was adapted into the acclaimed TV drama *Fallen Angel*, and the historical crime novels *The Ashes of London*, *The Silent Boy*, *The Scent of Death* and *The American Boy*, a No.1 *Sunday Times* bestseller and a 2005 Richard & Judy Book Club Choice.

He has won many awards, including the CWA John Creasey New Blood Dagger, an Edgar Scroll from the Mystery Writers of America, the CWA Ellis Peters Historical Award (the only author to win it three times) and the CWA's prestigious Diamond Dagger, awarded for sustained excellence in crime writing. He also writes for the *Spectator*.

He lives with his wife Caroline in the Forest of Dean.

🐦 @AndrewJRTaylor
www.andrew-taylor.co.uk

By the same author

The Ashes of London
The Silent Boy
The Scent of Death
The Anatomy Of Ghosts
Bleeding Heart Square
The American Boy

A Stain On The Silence
The Barred Window
The Raven On The Water

THE ROTH TRILOGY: FALLEN ANGEL
The Four Last Things
The Judgement Of Strangers
The Office Of The Dead

THE LYDMOUTH SERIES

THE BLAINES NOVELS

THE DOUGAL SERIES

ANDREW TAYLOR

Fireside Gothic

HarperCollins*Publishers*

HarperCollins*Publishers* Ltd
1 London Bridge Street,
London SE1 9GF

www.harpercollins.co.uk

This paperback edition 2017

1

First published in Great Britain by HarperCollins*Publishers* 2016

Copyright © Andrew Taylor 2016

Andrew Taylor asserts the moral right to
be identified as the author of this work

A catalogue record for this book is available from the British Library

ISBN: 978-0-00-817125-4

Set in Sabon by Palimpsest Book Production,
Falkirk, Stirlingshire

Printed and bound in the UK by CPI Group (UK) Ltd,
Croydon, CR0 4YY

For AKR, without whom . . .

Contents

BROKEN VOICES

1

Was there a ghost? Was there, in a manner of speaking, a murder?

Ask me these questions and I cannot answer a simple yes or no. I did not know at the time and now, more than forty years later, I am even less able to answer them. Perhaps an easier question is this: what exactly do I remember about Faraday and me in the few days we were together? Those years before the war seem so remote now. The First World War, that is, the one that was meant to end them all.

He and I didn't know each other long, not properly – four or five days, perhaps. And nights, of course. I suppose there must be records – a report in the local newspaper, surely, and a police file. Perhaps letters from Faraday's guardian. There must also have been correspondence between the school and my parents, but I found no trace of it after my mother died. We never spoke of it when she was alive, not directly, and my father wasn't able to speak about anything after they brought him back from France in 1915.

So – all I can really rely on is my memory. But memory may, paradoxically, make matters worse. It is not a passive record of what happens, though it may misleadingly give that impression. It plays an active role too, selecting and shaping the past. Memory speculates about itself; it ruminates and dreams, edits and deletes: over time, the fruits of these processes become the memories themselves and the entire process begins again.

So what does that make Faraday's fugitive notes? Or the man I saw in the arcade? Or even Mordred?

To take a minor example. I must have seen the view from the train as we went back to school over and over again. But in memory it is always winter, though I must often have seen it at other times of the year. All the different journeys have elided into one which, strictly speaking, never really happened at all.

The train comes north across the Fens. It's afternoon but the light is already fading rapidly from the endless bowl of the sky. The land is nearly as featureless – a plain of black mud stretching as far as the eyes can see. I stare out of the window, trying to find something to look at – a windmill, a hedge, a tree, a farm. Sometimes there is even a Fenlander. We used to call them Boggos.

I do not want to be on this train. Nor do I want to arrive at school. But there is no help in it: that's what I remember most of all, that the desolation outside the window mirrored the desolation within me.

That was nonsense, of course. They call it the Pathetic Fallacy, the belief that one can attach human emotions and thoughts to inanimate objects, even landscapes. I know that because Mr Ratcliffe explained it to Faraday and me. It may be a fallacy but sometimes fallacies have their own sort of truth.

When I look out of the window into the darkening world, I am looking for the two towers and dreading to find them. The sight of them means that the journey is coming to its end. One tower is taller than the other, and they are joined by the long, high-backed ridge of the nave.

4

The Fens diminish everything – people, buildings, trees. Everything except the Cathedral, which deals with the Fens on its own terms.

Most old English cathedrals have a school attached to them, often a King's School set up by Henry VIII at the Reformation. Ours was of no great size – perhaps a hundred pupils, some dayboys and some boarders, aged between nine and nineteen. Within the school was another school – technically, I believe a separate foundation: this was the Choir School, whose purpose was to educate the boys who sang in the Cathedral choir.

The Choir School was very small – twelve or fifteen boys. It was ruled by the Master of Music, Dr Atkinson, who was also the Cathedral organist. For much of the time, the Choir School boys mingled with the rest of us – they attended the same lessons and played the same games. But they were a race apart, nonetheless. They were liable to vanish unexpectedly to attend practice or perform their duties at one service or another. Their choir duties took precedence over everything else, even examinations. They had privileges and responsibilities that set them apart. They rarely talked of these except among themselves, and then in terms that were largely incomprehensible to outsiders, which added to the air of mystery that attached to them.

Faraday was a choirboy. He was thirteen years old. Before all this happened, I knew very little more about him, though we had attended the same school for years. I knew that he was supposed to be good at rugger. I knew he was the head of the Choir School, which meant that at services he wore a medallion engraved with the Cathedral's badge over his surplice, hanging from a ribbon around his neck. But I was more than a year older. He was in the form below mine and he lived in a different house. Our lives did not overlap.

The other thing that everyone knew about Faraday was that he had an exceptionally beautiful voice. Ours was the sort of school where you had to be good at sport, or work or music if you were to have a tolerable life. Faraday was good at everything, but especially good at singing.

I suppose I should also mention that I did not much like Faraday.

My parents were in India. They went there the week before my seventh birthday, leaving me in England. The climate was healthier for children, they said, and besides the schools were so much better. It was what many parents did in their situation: it was considered quite normal and in the best interests of the child. Perhaps it was. But I wished they had taken me with them. I still wish it.

During school holidays, I stayed with my aunt, the widowed sister of my father. My aunt was a kind woman. But she didn't know what to do with me and I didn't know what to do with her. She and my parents decided to send me to the King's School because it was only thirty miles from her house and it had the reputation of being a sound Christian establishment.

The school was a spartan place whose routine revolved around the Cathedral, even for those who were not in the choir. There was a good deal of bullying. Education of a sort was hammered into us. I made the best of it. What else was there to do?

I received regular letters from Quetta or Srinagar or New Delhi, written in my mother's careful, upright hand. Every year or so, my parents would come home on leave. I looked forward to these visits with anxiety and delight, as I dare say they did. Seeing my parents was always painful because they were not as they had been, and nor was I: we had become strangers to one another. We tried to make the most of it, but then they would be off again and whatever fragile intimacy we had achieved would trickle away, leaving behind more misleading memories. Still, I longed to see them. Hope always triumphed over experience.

The last time they came home, I was twelve. My father tried without success to teach me to fish; he wanted me to share his passion. My mother took me shopping with her and showed me off to her friends, who remained unimpressed. We went up to London for matinées at the theatre.

On one of these outings we had tea at the Charing Cross Hotel. I don't remember much about it except for one thing my mother said.

'You used to be such a chatterbox when you were little.' She smiled at me. 'Where did all the words go?'

My parents were coming home again. They would be here by mid-December in plenty of time for Christmas. My mother wrote that my father was planning to buy a motor car. If he did, they would drive over at the end of term and collect me.

The thought of my parents turning up at school in a motor car added a new element to my anticipation. At that time cars were uncommon, especially in the Fens. I imagined my parents driving up in an enormous, gleaming equipage worthy of Mr Toad in *The Wind in the Willows* and sweeping me away before the whole school. Like a fool, I boasted to my friends of this triumph to come, which was tempting fate.

I did not have long to enjoy it. In my mother's next letter she wrote that they had been obliged to change their plans. They would not be able to come home this year after all.

'It's nothing to worry about, darling,' she wrote, 'but I've been a little under the weather lately, and the doctor says it would be better to leave it until next year. Daddy and I are so disappointed, though we know you will have a wonderful time at Christmas with Auntie Mary. And next year, we shall try to come home for longer.'

I know the reason now. My mother had just discovered she was pregnant. Of course, neither she nor my father ever talked about it to me, but it was easy enough to work out when my sister was born the following May.

Fifteen years is a long gap to leave between children. Perhaps my parents found it hard to conceive another child. Perhaps my sister was an accident. Not that it matters now. But it is strange to think that, if my sister had never existed, none of this would have happened and I would have been quite a different person now. And as for Faraday . . .

'Try not to mind too much, darling,' my mother's letter ended. 'With fondest love.'

Nevertheless, I looked forward to Christmas. If nothing else it meant getting away from school and going to a warm house where there were four meals a day and I was never left hungry for long. My aunt knew little about boys but she knew a great deal about creature comforts. The vicar's son would be home from school, which meant that for at least part of the time I would have someone to go about with. And there would be presents – and perhaps more generous ones this year because my parents would feel I deserved consolation.

Two days before the end of term, Mr Treadwell, my housemaster, sent a boy to fetch me. He was a small, harassed man, a bachelor, who didn't care for boys or anything else except geology, which was his passion.

'There's been a difficulty,' he said, staring at the fire; he never looked at you if he could help it. 'I'm sorry to say that your aunt is unwell.'

He paused. I did not dare interrupt him with a question. My housemaster believed boys should hold their tongues unless asked to speak. He had a vicious temper, too – we never knew how far he would go when roused.

'She's in hospital, in fact. Pneumonia, I'm afraid.' He was still staring at the fire, but I saw the tip of his tongue emerge, lizard-like, from between his lips. 'We must remember her in our prayers. Must we not?'

I recognized my cue. 'Yes, sir.'

'We must hope for a full recovery,' he went on. 'Not a good time of year to be ill. But still.'

'What about Christmas, sir?' I blurted out.

My housemaster turned his head and glared at me. But he must have remembered the circumstances, for when he spoke his voice was almost gentle.

'You will have to stay at school,' he said. 'I have arranged for you to lodge with Mr Ratcliffe. It will be best for all concerned.'

2

Christmas that year fell on a Wednesday. 'Wednesday's Child is full of woe,' shrieked one small boy over and over again as he ran round the playground, until one of the bullies of the Fifth Form pushed him over and made him cry instead.

The school broke up two days earlier, on Monday. It was strange to watch the familiar routines unfolding and not be part of them: the station fly taking boys to the railway station by relays; the steady stream of parents, always a matter of enormous sociological interest; the boys queueing to shake hands with Mr Treadwell.

At that stage I was not the only one to stay – two other boys at Treadwell's did not leave with the rest on Monday. For an hour or two, we revelled in undisputed possession of the few amenities the house afforded – the billiards table with torn baize, for example, and the two armchairs that leaked horsehair by the common room fire. There was a sense of holiday so we talked loudly and laughed a great deal to show what fun we were having.

On Christmas Eve, however, these boys left as well, collected one by one by their parents. Mr Treadwell's suitcases stood in the hall. He shook hands with Matron, who was going to her married sister in Huntingdon, and tipped the maids.

Finally, only Mr Treadwell and I were left. He looked at his watch. 'The taxi will be here soon. I'll take you over to Mr Ratcliffe's now.'

My trunk, packed and corded, was staying at Treadwell's with my tuckbox. But I had been given a small suitcase, in which Matron had put those things she thought I would need, and I had a satchel containing a few personal possessions. I followed Treadwell into the College, which was the name given to the Cathedral close.

The College was, and for all I know still is, a world apart with its own laws and customs. Every evening at 7 p.m., the great gates were closed, and the place turned in on itself for the night. Its boundaries were those of the mediaeval monastery, as were many of its buildings where the Cathedral dignitaries lived and where the houses and classrooms of the school were.

Mr Ratcliffe lived at one end of what had been the Sacrist's Lodging. He was a bachelor who had taught at the school for many years and who now lived in semi-retirement in a grace-and-favour house granted to him by the Dean and Chapter. He was still active, though he must have been in his early seventies, and regularly attended school functions and sometimes took classes when masters were away or ill. Unlike many of his former colleagues on the staff, he was not a clergyman.

'It is most kind of Mr Ratcliffe to invite you to stay,' Mr Treadwell told me on my way over. 'You must try not to disturb him too much.'

'How long will I be there, sir?'

'It depends on your aunt's health. I've asked her doctor to write to Mr Ratcliffe and he will pass on the news to you. If she's well enough, she may want you home after Christmas.' He must have seen my face for he hurried on,

11

'But I advise you not to raise your hopes too high. Pneumonia is a very serious illness. Very serious indeed.'

'Will she . . . will she die?'

'God willing, no. But pneumonia can be fatal. You must pray for her.'

The Sacrist's Lodging had been built against the northern boundary wall of the monastery. Most of the doors and windows faced inwards. If you looked out, you saw the Cathedral blocking out the earth and sky.

Mr Ratcliffe answered Mr Treadwell's knock. He was a tall man, quite bald apart from two tufts of white hair above his ears. He generally wore knickerbockers and a tweed jacket, stiff with age, with leather elbow patches.

He was very brisk and businesslike on that first meeting – I felt that my plight deserved a little more sympathy than he gave it. He showed me over the house, with Mr Treadwell hovering behind us and making the occasional clucking sound designed to express approval and gratitude.

The tour didn't take long. Downstairs, at the front, there was a sitting room dominated by a grand piano which occupied almost half the floor space. The air was stuffy with pipe smoke, which filled the air with a fine, blue-grey fog. There were books everywhere. They were shelved in the orthodox manner along the walls. They stood in piles under the piano and on the piano. They lined the mantelpiece and colonized the shadowy corners.

A tortoiseshell cat was asleep on one of the chairs. It opened one eye, looked at us, and shut it again.

'That's Mordred,' Mr Ratcliffe said, looking directly at me for the first time. 'I'd be careful with him, if I were you.'

'Mordred?' Mr Treadwell said. 'An unusual name for a cat.'

'In *Le Morte d'Arthur*,' Mr Ratcliffe said, 'Mordred

betrays his uncle the King. Not a nice man. I regret to say that Mordred is not nice either, hence the name.'

'In that case, I'm surprised you keep him.'

'I've had him since he was very young. I must make the best of him now, just as he must make the best of me.'

Apart from the sitting room, the other rooms downstairs were a kitchen and dining room, dark little rooms with small windows, heavily barred, overlooking the bustle of the High Street.

'One washes here,' Mr Ratcliffe said, gesturing towards the kitchen sink. 'I am afraid there's no bathroom. The lavatory is outside in the yard. If I need a bath, my neighbours kindly let me use theirs. I have had a word with them, and they have no objection to extending their hospitality to you. Of course, I try not to trouble them very often if I can possibly help it.'

'Splendid!' Mr Treadwell said.

Upstairs there were only two rooms. The door of the one at the front remained closed – 'My bedroom,' Mr Ratcliffe explained, with an odd, apologetic twitch of his face.

The one at the back was mine. Like the kitchen and dining room below, it overlooked the High Street. It was low-ceilinged with two beds and a quantity of dark furniture designed for less cramped quarters. The window was small and barred, like the ones downstairs. It faced north and let in very little daylight. The air smelled damp.

Mr Treadwell poked his head into the gloom. 'Splendid,' he said. 'Splendid.' He withdrew and clattered downstairs.

'I – er – I hope you'll be comfortable.' Mr Ratcliffe glanced round the room. 'Mrs Thing made up the bed on the left. She must have thought you would be more comfortable there.'

'Who's Mrs Thing, sir?' I asked, and my voice emerged as a loud croak.

'The woman who does – she comes in three times a week to clean. And so on.' He frowned, as if trying to recall what she did do. 'I stay out of her way myself.'

'Is she really called Mrs Thing?'

Mr Ratcliffe appeared to give the matter serious consideration. 'Well, no. Or not that I know of. But I can never remember her name. Indeed, I cannot be sure that I ever knew it. So I call her Mrs Thing instead.'

We went back downstairs. Mr Treadwell was waiting in the hall and frowning at his watch.

'I haven't mentioned your meals,' he said. 'Mr Ratcliffe makes his own arrangements. But you will find bread and milk in the kitchen, I understand.'

'And tea,' Mr Ratcliffe put in. 'And butter and jam. Help yourself.'

'That's very kind of you, Mr Ratcliffe.' Treadwell turned back to me. 'You will take your lunch and tea at Mr Veal's house. You know where that is? Beside the Porta.'

'Yes, sir.' The Porta was the great gateway at the far end of the College. Mr Veal was the head verger of the Cathedral, a tyrant who waged an endless war against the boys of the King's School.

'I am sure Mrs Veal will look after you.' Mr Treadwell retreated towards the door. 'It only remains for me to wish you both a very happy Christmas. Goodbye – I must rush.'

With that, Mr Treadwell was gone. The door slammed behind him. I never saw him again, as it happens, a circumstance I do not regret. Not in itself.

Mr Ratcliffe led the way into the sitting room, saying over his shoulder, 'A train, no doubt. They wait for no man, do they?'

I followed him into the room and stared about me. I dare say I looked a little forlorn.

'You could read a book, I suppose,' he suggested. 'That's

what I generally do. Or perhaps you would like to unpack. You mustn't mind me – just as you please.'

I was standing near the chair on which Mordred lay. The first I knew of this was when I felt an acute pain in the back of my left hand. I cried out. When I looked down, the cat had folded its forelegs and was staring up at me with amber eyes, flecked with green. There were two spots of blood on my hand. I sucked them away.

'Mordred!' Mr Ratcliffe said. 'I do apologize.'

Freedom is an unsatisfactory thing. I had longed for the end of term, to the end of the chafing restrictions of school. But when I had freedom, I did not know what to do with it.

Mr Ratcliffe set no boundaries whatsoever on my conduct. In this he was perhaps wiser than I realized at the time. But he made it clear – wordlessly, and with the utmost courtesy – that he and Mordred had their own lives, their own routines, and that he did not wish me to disturb them if at all possible.

On that first day, I went into the town during the afternoon. During term time, we boys were not allowed to leave a College except when specifically authorized – to walk to the playing field, for example, or to visit the home of a dayboy, or to go to one of the few shops that the school authorities had licensed us to patronize. We were allowed to go shopping only on Saturday afternoons, and only in pairs.

So – to ramble the streets at will on Christmas Eve, to go into shops on a whim: it should have been glorious. Instead it was cold and boring. The hurrying people making last-minute purchases emphasized my own isolation. Everywhere I looked there were signs of excitement, of anticipation, of secular pleasures to come. I had a strong suspicion that Mr Ratcliffe would not celebrate Christmas

15

at all, except perhaps by going to church more often than usual.

I tried to buy a packet of cigarettes in a tobacconist's, but the man knew I was at the King's School by my cap and refused to serve me. I had a cup of tea and an iced bun in a café, where mothers and daughters stared at me with, I thought, both curiosity and pity.

In the end, there was nothing for it but to go back to the College, to Mr Ratcliffe's. At the Sacrist's Lodging, his door was unlocked. I hung up my coat and cap and went into the sitting room.

Mr Ratcliffe wasn't there. But a boy was sitting in Mordred's chair, with Mordred on his lap. He had a long thin head, and his ears stood out from his skull. His front teeth were prominent and slightly crooked.

The cat was purring. They both looked at me.

'Hello,' said the boy. 'I'm Faraday.'

3

That was the start of my acquaintance with Faraday. It's strange that such a brief relationship should have had such a profound effect on both of us. He was very thin – all skin and bone – but there was nothing remarkable in that. The school food was appalling and few of us grew fat on it. Some people called him 'Rabbit' because of his teeth.

The front door opened. Mr Ratcliffe came into the house. 'Ah – there you are. I see you've met Faraday. But perhaps you two are already friends?'

I shook my head. Faraday continued stroking the cat.

'As you see, he has already established a friendship with Mordred. How long it will last is another matter.' Mr Ratcliffe sat down and began to ream his pipe. 'Mrs Thing is making up the other bed.'

'He's staying here?' I said. 'But—'

'I'm not in the choir any more,' Faraday interrupted. 'That's why I'm here.'

I noticed two things: that Faraday's face had gone very red, and that his voice started on a high pitch but descended rapidly into a croak.

'Yes,' Mr Ratcliffe said, tapping his pipe on the hearth to remove the last of the dottle. 'Poor chap. Faraday's voice has broken. Pity it should happen just before Christmas, but there it is. Dr Atkinson decided it would be better not to take a chance: so here he is.'

Even then I knew there must be more to it than this. The brisk jollity of Mr Ratcliffe's voice told me that, and so did Faraday's face. Even if Faraday's voice had reached the point where it could not be trusted, they could have let him stay with them, let him walk with the choir on Christmas morning with his badge of honour around his neck.

Faraday looked up. 'They chucked me out,' he said. 'It's not fair.'

At the time I pitied only myself. Now I realize that all of us in that house deserved pity for one reason or another.

Faraday's voice had betrayed him. His greatest ally had become the traitor within. He had lost not just his place in the choir but also his sense of who he was. Mr Ratcliffe must have loathed the necessity to share his house with two boys, disturbing his quiet routines and upsetting his cat. It didn't occur to me until much later that he was probably very poor. He must have received some money from the school for housing us. Perhaps he had felt in no position to refuse. After all, he was old and alone; he lived a grace-and-favour life in a grace-and-favour house.

Faraday and I went to the verger's house at six in the evening, where Mrs Veal gave us Welsh rarebit, blancmange and a glass of milk. We ate in the Veals' parlour, a stiff little room smelling of polish and soot. On the mantelpiece was a mynah bird, stuffed and attached to a twig, encased in a glass dome.

On that occasion we saw only Mrs Veal, apart from near the end of the meal when Mr Veal came in from the Cathedral, still in his verger's cassock; he wished us good evening in a gruff voice and opened the door of a wall cupboard. I glimpsed two rows of hooks within, holding keys of various sizes.

'Enjoy your supper,' he told us, and went into the kitchen, where we heard him talking to his wife.

Faraday rose from his chair, crossed the room to the cupboard and opened the door.

'Dozens of keys,' he whispered. 'And all with labels. It's the keys for everywhere.'

I pretended not to be interested. 'Sit down,' I said. 'Or he'll catch you.'

That night I heard Faraday crying.

I remember in my first term at school I would lie in bed, listening for other boys crying and stuffing my handkerchief in my own mouth in an attempt to muffle my tears. There were about twenty of us huddled under thin blankets in a high-ceilinged dormitory, the windows wide open winter or summer. Sometimes one of the older boys would round on one of the weeping children.

'Bloody blubber,' he would whisper, and the rest of us would repeat the words over and over again, like an incantation, lest we be accused of blubbing as well. Little savages.

But that had been years ago. I wasn't a kid any more and nor was Faraday.

'Faraday?' I murmured.

There was instant silence.

'Are you crying?'

'I've got a cold.'

It was the usual excuse, transparently false.

'What is it?' I said. And waited.

'Everything. Bloody everything.'

We lay there without speaking. The room was not quite dark – the curtains were thin and the light from a High Street lamp leaked into the room.

'But it's my bloody voice really,' he went on. 'Everything would have been all right if it hadn't been for that.'

'That's rot,' I said, with the loftiness of fourteen to thirteen. 'Everyone's voice has to break sometime, unless you're a girl. You don't want to be a girl, do you?'

This was an attempt at comfort but it seemed only to make Faraday start crying again.

'Come on,' I said. 'You can't just blub.'

'You don't understand. I was going to sing the Christmas anthem. There's a solo, you see, and it's usually the head chorister that does it, and the Bishop gives him a special present afterwards. Some money.'

'How much?' I said.

'Five pounds.'

I whistled. 'For a bit of singing? That's stupid.'

'No, it's not.' Faraday's voice rose in volume and, suddenly, in pitch. 'It's a tradition. They've been doing it for hundreds of years. Some old bishop left money in his will for it. And now Hampson will do it instead.'

'Don't talk so loud. The Rat will hear you.'

'It's lovely, too,' Faraday whispered.

Lovely was not a word we used much. 'What is?'

'The anthem. It's for Christmas Day. It's called "Jubilate Deo", and we only sing it on Christmas morning.'

Rejoice to God. Both of us had enough Latin to translate that.

'All right,' I said. 'It's beastly to lose five quid. But is it that bad? I mean, it was never yours in the first place.'

Faraday started crying again. I was spending Christmas with a cry-baby. I curled myself into a ball to conserve heat and thought how perfectly miserable everything was. Or rather, how perfectly miserable I was. Boys are selfish little brutes. While I was wallowing in self-pity, however, my curiosity was still stirring.

'Look here,' I said, 'I can see it's a shame your voice is

broken and all that. But why are you like this about it? And why are you here?'

The snuffling continued. It was getting on my nerves.

'Why aren't you still at the Choir House? Or why didn't Dr Atkinson send you home to your people?'

'My parents are dead,' Faraday said, and the waterworks increased in force.

That jolted me out of my own misery. I knew what it was to miss your parents, you see, and even I could imagine how infinitely worse it would be if you could never, ever see them again. Or not until after you died and went to heaven, assuming heaven was real, which in those days I still considered to be a sporting possibility.

'So where do you go in the holidays?'

'To my guardian's, in Wales. But this year he's had to go away. So I was going to stay with the Atkinsons until he comes back.'

This deepened the mystery. 'Then why aren't you there now?'

'It's because of Hampson Minor. Bloody Hampson.'

'Yes, you said – he'll get the five quid because he's going to sing the anthem, and I suppose he's the new head of the choir, too.'

Faraday's bed creaked. 'It's not that. He had a postal order from his uncle. Ten bob.'

I whistled softly in the darkness. Not in the same league as the Bishop's five pounds, but still pretty decent. I wished my aunt would give me ten shillings sometimes.

'He was swanking about it all the time. The postal order and being head of the choir and the Bishop's money. He just went on and on and everyone was sucking up to him. He said he was going to buy a big cake from Fowler's for everyone. I just wanted to kick him. You know what he's like.'

I only knew Hampson Minor by sight. He was a fat,

pink-faced boy with small delicate features and prominent lips. When he sang, he made his lips into a perfect O.

'He left the postal order on the floor. It must have fallen – it was with his exercise book. So I – I picked it up and put it in my pocket.'

'You stole it?'

'No,' Faraday wailed. 'I was just going to keep it for a bit, until he found he had lost it, and then give it back. To teach him a lesson. That's all. Honestly.'

I didn't know whether he was telling the truth. I didn't know then and I don't know now.

'But he told Dr Atkinson it was gone, and Dr Atkinson made us all empty our pockets and open our boxes.' Faraday paused for a long moment. 'And they found it.'

I didn't know what to say. Stealing was a sackable offence at the King's School.

'I was going to give it back, I swear it. I didn't know he'd tell old Atky straight away. The rotten sneak.'

'What will happen?' The scale of the offence awed me. 'Will they chuck you out?'

'I don't know,' Faraday whimpered. 'I just don't know. And even if they let me stay, everyone will know. So that'll be almost as bad. And then there's Hampson's brother. I'd be in the senior school.'

I was beginning to take a warped pleasure in having a ringside seat to the tragedy which was unfolding on such a grand scale. Faraday, the golden boy, had lost his singing voice, his five pounds and his pre-eminent role as head choirboy. He was now faced with a hideous pair of alternatives: if he was expelled from school he faced a lifetime of shame and whatever punishment his guardian cared to mete out; if he was allowed to stay, his remaining years at the school would be made a living hell, particularly by Hampson Major, a gorilla of a boy who played second row forward in the First XV, and who had a well-deserved reputation for brutality verging on sadism. He was bad enough as a casual tyrant over anyone smaller than himself. He would be a figure of nightmare if he chose to persecute you seriously.

'God,' I said as the full horror of Faraday's situation hit me. 'You poor bloody kid.'

He was crying again, softly, continuously, a sort of moaning and sobbing that at last moved me to pity, and even to a desire to help.

'Look here, Rabbit,' I said. It was the first time I called him by his nickname. 'Perhaps it won't be as bad as you think.'

The crying stopped. I heard Faraday's ragged breathing.

A sense of power filled me. He believed I might be able to help, and that almost made me believe it too.

'Listen,' I said. 'We'll think of something. I promise.'

4

For every child, I think, there must be a day when
Christmas loses its magic. By 'magic' I don't mean an
unquestioning belief in Father Christmas or a foolish
attachment to improbable ideas about reindeer and chim-
neys and so on. Nor does the magic I mean reside in the
religious connotations of the day, though of course, for
many people, the one cannot be separated from the other
and Christmas is always the birthday of Jesus. I envy them.

The magic has more to do with a sense that this is a
special day, when nothing is allowed to go wrong. When
you are given presents, good food and a licence to enjoy
luxuries and activities that lie beyond the reach of most
of us for 364 days of the year. When people are kind to
each other and there is a sense of holiday.

The illusion is strongest in infancy, and most of us lose
it gradually during childhood. But we cling to it, we fool
ourselves, as long as possible. In the end there has to come
a day when we are forced finally to acknowledge the truth:
that Christmas is a day like any other, potentially neither
better nor worse, but actually almost always worse because
it trails in its wake the ghosts of its lost magic.

For me it was that Christmas at Sacrist's Lodging: that's

when at last I accepted that a Christmas Day could be as miserable as any other.

The morning began when we went downstairs to find Mr Ratcliffe making tea in the kitchen. On the mat by the back door were the hind legs and tail of a mouse; Mordred had already celebrated Christmas in his own special way.

We wished each other happy Christmas. Mr Ratcliffe was wearing an ancient suit, once a uniform black but now shiny and even green in places, in honour of the day.

He gave us cups of strong, sweet tea, with very little milk in it.

'I thought we would go to Matins and then the Eucharist afterwards,' he said. 'I don't usually eat before taking communion, if I can avoid it. It seems rude somehow.'

'What about Christmas dinner, sir?' I asked in alarm.

'Mrs Veal will have something for you at lunchtime, I'm sure. Don't worry about that. I'll have mine at the Deanery.' He hesitated, and I guessed that he had remembered the Dean also entertained to lunch those members of the choir who had not left immediately after the morning services. 'We'll meet again in the evening, I expect, when you are back from the Veals'.'

Mordred sauntered into the room and picked up the remains of the mouse. He wandered into the hall.

'I'll let him outside, shall I?' Faraday said in a rush.

He dashed after the cat. I heard him fumbling with the front door with clumsy urgency, as though trying to escape.

I suppose that was what we all wanted – Faraday, myself and even, perhaps, poor Mr Ratcliffe: to escape.

There was no snow that Christmas.

It was very cold. The grass around the Cathedral was a hard, sparkling white, and frost clung to the leafless branches of trees and bushes. The flagged paths were treacherous – any moisture had turned to ice overnight.

Mr Ratcliffe strode slowly along, his stick tapping the pavement. 'Beautiful,' he said over his shoulder to Faraday and me, trailing behind him. 'Quite beautiful.'

The College was crowded with groups of people making their way to church. On Christmas morning, the Cathedral had one of its largest congregations of the year, even though the King's School wasn't there to swell its ranks.

We sat in the presbytery, the rows of seats on either side near the high altar, to the east of the choir stalls. Above us were the pipes of the organ and the wooden cabin of the organ loft, clinging like a growth to one bay of the choir aisle.

I don't remember much about the services except that they seemed to go on for ever and that I seriously thought I might faint or even die from hunger. It must have been hell for poor Faraday to see the choir processing through the chancel gates, filing in two by two, and peeling off into their stalls in the choir.

Hampson Minor led them in, with the head boy's medal resting on his surplice. He looked larger and pinker than before, as if his promotion had inflated him a little further than nature had done already. His eyes darted about the chancel. I guessed he was looking for Faraday. As he turned to lead his file into the choir stalls, he found us. For a fraction of a second he paused. Beside me, Faraday stiffened like a threatened animal.

The moment was gone. The choir flowed smoothly into the stalls and the service began.

I had attended many services in the Cathedral – the school used it as its chapel – but I had never been there on Christmas Day. The Bishop was there enthroned, a gaudy, overstuffed doll with his mitre and crozier. Each seat was full.

I concentrated on not fainting from starvation; on standing, sitting and kneeling; on mouthing the hymns in a soundless but visually convincing way, a skill I had perfected in my first term; and, most of all, on thinking about what Mrs Veal might provide for our Christmas dinner.

But I did notice when the choir sang the anthem, the 'Jubilate Deo'. The first part was sung by Hampson Minor alone: I could see him, his mouth an O of surprise, his face pinker than ever with the effort. Then, one by one, the rest of the choir joined in, and then the organ thundered into life and they all made a dreadful racket until it was time for us to kneel down and pray again.

Faraday leaned towards me undercover of shuffling as the entire congregation was sinking to its knees.

'He muffed it, the silly ass,' he muttered. 'The end of bar sixteen. He couldn't hold the E flat.'

For the first time, I saw Faraday smile.

Mrs Veal had bought us Christmas cards, and I felt guilty that we had not thought to do the same for our hosts. Mr Veal carved the beef and the ham. We ate late – Mr Veal had plenty to keep him busy after a service – but Mrs Veal took pity on us and gave us a preliminary helping of Yorkshire pudding and gravy.

In his capacity as head verger, Mr Veal was a figure who inspired fear and mockery in equal parts. Now, however, Faraday and I saw the domestic Veal, his dignity put aside with his verger's gown. In private, with a good meal inside him, a glass of port in one hand and his pipe in the other, he revealed himself as almost genial. I remember he told us a story about one canon who grew so fat that it was only with difficulty that he could squeeze into his stall; in the end they had to make a special chair for him. He laughed so hard that his face became purple.

The Christmas dinner was the only time that I saw Faraday looking really happy. The Veals were kindly people: they gave us food, warmth and a welcome. Perhaps there was a little Christmas magic after all.

'A lot of queer stories about the Cathedral,' said Mr Veal on his third glass of port. 'And I could tell you a few, if I had a mind to. Have you heard about the bells?'

'But there aren't any,' Faraday said. 'Not in the Cathedral. Only the clock chimes.'

'Ah. Not now. But there were bells, once upon a time.'

'Get along with you, George,' said Mrs Veal. 'Save it for later. I need to clear the table and these boys need to get back or Mr Ratcliffe will be wondering where they are.'

'He knows about it, all right,' Mr Veal says.

'Who does, dear?'

'Mr Ratcliffe. He knows about the stories.'

5

In the evening of Christmas Day, we made mugs of cocoa together and sat around the fire in the sitting room at the Sacrist's Lodging. Like Mr Veal, Mr Ratcliffe had drunk a few glasses of wine with his dinner and was unusually expansive.

Mordred condescended to join us. He sat on the chair nearest the fire, head erect, with his back to us. It was Mordred who started Mr Ratcliffe on ghosts.

'I am afraid he's a little stand-offish today. You wouldn't think it, but he doesn't like being left alone in the house. We abandoned him for most of the day and now he's sulking.'

'He doesn't look as if he'd notice if he was alone or not.' My scratches still rankled. 'I don't think he likes people.'

'You may be right,' Mr Ratcliffe said, patting his pockets for his oilskin tobacco pouch. 'But he finds us convenient, and not just for food and warmth. Perhaps we help to ward off the ghosts.'

'Ghosts?' Faraday said. 'What ghosts?' In those three words his voice modulated from a rumble to a squeak.

'Do you know any stories about them, sir?' I said. 'Will you tell us one?'

'Mordred used to see the ghost next door,' Mr Ratcliffe said, nodding towards the party wall that divided this part of the Sacrist's Lodging from the other. 'He was just a kitten then, and he didn't know what to make of it. In fact, that's why he lives with me. He kept coming over here to get away from the ghost, and in the end the Precentor said I might as well keep him.'

'Have you seen it, sir?' I asked. By this stage of my life I had my doubts about the existence of God but I was more than willing to keep an open mind about ghosts.

'Yes, several times over the years.' Mr Ratcliffe had given up on his pockets. Still talking, he rose from his chair and eventually discovered the pouch wedged between the seat and the arm. 'Of course I didn't realize it was a ghost at first.'

'What did it look like?' Faraday said.

'Like a cat.'

'A cat?'

'Yes, a little grey cat. One used to see it in the corner of the big room upstairs occasionally. Quite harmless. It's probably still there, for all I know. It comes and goes.'

'What did it do?' I said.

'Nothing very much. It just sat there. Sometimes you saw it moving across the room. You always glimpsed it out of the corner of your eye, if you know what I mean. But Mordred was different – he saw it directly. He behaved as if it was another cat, arching his back and so on. But then it simply terrified him, and he wouldn't stay in the same house. So he moved here, next door. But it was odd, really – the grey cat never seemed to notice his existence at all.'

'Perhaps it thought Mordred was the ghost,' Faraday suggested with a giggle. 'Perhaps he was trying to pretend Mordred wasn't there.'

Mr Ratcliffe struck a match and paused, considering

the remark, the flame flickering over the bowl of the pipe.

'Anything is possible, I suppose,' he said at last, and sucked the flame deep into the pipe. 'We may haunt ghosts as much as the other way round.'

'Or they may not even know we're there,' I put in, feeling that Faraday was having too much of the limelight.

'Some of the time they certainly know we're there.' The light was dim and Mr Ratcliffe's features disintegrated in a cloud of smoke. 'Or some of them do. That was undoubtedly the case with the blue lady. She always behaved very cordially to me. On the other hand, one should not generalize from the particular.' He must have seen our expressions, for he added hastily, 'I mean that one ghost who behaves like that does not necessarily mean that they all do.'

'Please, sir,' Faraday said, sounding like a little boy, 'who is the blue lady?'

'She is at the Deanery,' Mr Ratcliffe said. 'I used to go there a good deal when I was younger.' He glanced at the piano that dominated the room. 'Not in this Dean's time, or even the one before. There was a lady – the Dean's daughter, as it happens – who played the violin and wanted an accompanist.'

'Was she the blue lady?' I asked.

'She was entirely flesh and blood.' Mr Ratcliffe gave a cough. He turned away from us and blew his nose. 'But I often went up to the Deanery drawing room in those days, and I sometimes met the blue lady on the stairs.'

'How did you know she was a ghost, sir? Could she have been someone staying there?'

'Oh no. She wore a dress with panniers under the skirt. Eighteenth century, I imagine. Besides, I encountered her on one occasion when I was with Miss . . . with the Dean's daughter, and she didn't see her.'

Faraday leaned forward, his head resting on his hands. 'What happened, sir? Did she speak? Did you?'

'No,' Mr Ratcliffe said. 'We hadn't been introduced, you see. So I bowed – and she bobbed a small curtsy. It was always like that – I must have seen her three or four times. The last time I glanced back and she was looking up at me. I thought she might be going to say something. But she didn't.'

'Did you ask the Dean about her?' I said.

Mr Ratcliffe shook his head. 'It would not have been wise. But I did ask his daughter if the Deanery was said to be haunted, and she said no, but that her mother had been obliged to dismiss a housemaid who was making up silly stories to frighten the other servants. Stories about a lady in an old-fashioned dress.'

Faraday's mouth had fallen open in amazement. He looked more like a rabbit than ever.

'It all seems so pointless, sir,' I said. 'The cat – the blue lady.'

'Why does it have to have a point?' Mr Ratcliffe said. 'Which is to say, a purpose that we in our present situation are able to understand. It's true that in some cases one can speculate about that. In other words, there may be a possible factual basis that might underlie a ghostly phenomenon.'

'He means there is a real story to explain the ghost,' I told Faraday, as much to display my superior understanding as to enlighten his ignorance.

'One or two of our own ghosts come into that category. Take Mr Goldsworthy, for example. On the other hand, the real story may not explain the ghost – it may be the other way round: that the ghost is our way of trying to explain something puzzling or disturbing that actually occurred. Something we somehow create ourselves.'

Mr Ratcliffe paused. He peered through his pipe smoke

at Faraday and me. He had been a schoolmaster all his life and he knew boys.

'It is getting late,' he said. 'You two should go to bed.'

'But, sir,' Faraday said. 'What about Mr Goldsworthy?'

Mr Ratcliffe smiled at him. 'I'll tell you about him tomorrow evening.'

'Oh, sir.' Faraday sounded about nine years old. I scowled at him, though I was as keen to hear about Mr Goldsworthy as he was.

We said our good nights. Mr Ratcliffe stayed by the fire, smoking and reading. I went outside to use the lavatory while Faraday carried the cups into the kitchen and stacked them in the sink.

It was colder than ever outside. The air chilled my throat and tingled in my nose. Above the black ridge of the Cathedral was the arch of the sky, where the stars gleamed white and silver and pale blue: they seemed to vibrate with the cold, shivering in heaven.

Afterwards, I went upstairs. Faraday went outside in his turn. By the time he came upstairs, I was already in bed and reading my book, a novel called *Beric the Briton* by G. A. Henty. I ignored him while he undressed. I heard his bedsprings creak as he climbed into bed and the sharp intake of breath as the cold, slightly damp sheets touched his skin.

'I say,' Faraday said. 'Can I ask you something?'

I lowered the book. 'What?'

He was lying on his side, curled up with his knees nearly at his chin. All I could see of him was his face. He looked more rabbit-like than ever.

'Did you hear it outside? The – the singing, or whatever it was?'

'What are you talking about?'

'It was when I came out of the bog,' he said.

'Perhaps the Rat was having a sing-song,' I said. 'He

33

got drunk on the Dean's wine. It was obvious, the way he was going on this evening.'

'It wasn't him, honestly – it came from outside, from over there.'

Faraday's hand emerged from under the covers and pointed to the right of our beds: towards the College, towards the Cathedral.

'Someone coming home from a party,' I said.

'It wasn't like that.' He was frowning. 'It was just four notes, very high-pitched and far away.'

Very quietly, Faraday sang them to me: La-la-la-la. The third la was longer than the others. His voice behaved itself for once, and the notes sounded pure and true. As far as I could tell.

'You sure you didn't hear it?'

'Of course I'm sure. Go to sleep.'

He sang the notes again, even more quietly. 'It's in a major key, I think. Starts on an F sharp, perhaps?'

'Shut up, will you?'

I reached up and turned off the gas at the bracket on the wall.

'Whatever it is,' he said to the darkness, 'it's meant to be happy but it's going to be a sad tune.'

I lay awake listening to the sounds of the night, wondering whether Faraday would start crying again. He hadn't mentioned the business with the postal order during the day but it must always have been there, squatting in the forefront of his mind like a toad and waiting for its moment to spring. His plight made mine seem trivial by comparison, which I suppose was another reason I didn't like him very much.

Faraday's breathing slowed and fell into a regular rhythm. I heard Mr Ratcliffe locking up and coming up the stairs. The Cathedral clock tolled the hours and the quarters. The clock was in the west tower, not the shorter central tower. It had a modest chime for such a large church, like a big man with a small, high voice. We boys called it 'Little Willy'.

The silence deepened. Once, as I was dropping off to sleep, I thought I heard again, at the very edge of my range of hearing, the four high notes that Faraday had sung to me. La-la-la-la.

6

For most of Boxing Day, we were left to our own devices. Mr Ratcliffe went out after breakfast to call on a former servant at the King's School who now lived in one of the almshouses attached to the parish church. He would go directly on from there to have lunch with an old friend in a village a mile away from the town. He did not expect to be back until evening.

Time passed slowly for us. We were in a sort of limbo, neither at home nor at school. Faraday and I kept together because we had no one else to be with and nothing else to do.

In the morning we stayed at the Sacrist's Lodging, reading under the disdainful gaze of Mordred. I finished *Beric the Briton* and looked along Mr Ratcliffe's shelves for something else to read. Most of his books were about boring things like music or architecture. There was some poetry, equally boring, and the sort of books we had at school, like Shakespeare. In the end I had to settle for *Oliver Twist*.

Faraday irritated me more than usual. He couldn't stay still for a moment. He moved around the room, fiddling with the ornaments and looking at the pictures, most of which were engravings of old buildings.

He sat down on the stool and raised the lid of the grand piano.

'Do you play?' I said.

'Yes.' He pulled back his cuffs and spread his fingers over the keyboard. A ripple of notes burst into the room.

Naturally he played the piano, I thought: bloody Faraday could do everything and do it well.

'God!' he said in quite a different voice. 'It's awful.'

'What is?'

'The piano. Can't you hear? It's awfully out of tune. I bet it's warped.'

'Good,' I said, returning to page two of *Oliver Twist*. 'At least that'll stop you playing it.'

Whether the piano was in tune or not was all the same to me. I have never understood music and its power to affect some people so profoundly.

He closed the lid with a bang.

Faraday and I couldn't afford to quarrel, or not for long. We needed each other too much. We went into the town, though the shops were closed, and walked the long way round to the Veals' house beside the Porta.

Mrs Veal welcomed us like a pair of prodigal sons – she had grown used to us now, I suppose, and saw us for what we were: a pair of lost children who needed feeding up. She gave us cold beef and cold ham, and as much mashed potato as we could cram into ourselves. Then came apple pie, followed by cups of tea so densely packed with sugar and cream you could almost stand your spoon up in it.

For the first time we saw Mr Veal in his shirtsleeves. He was in a jovial mood, with a glass or two of beer beside him. This time was a sort of holiday to him, he explained. For the Cathedral's rhythms built up to the great feasts of the church, like Christmas; but after these climaxes there came lulls. The daily round of services continued, but on a reduced basis. The choir was on holiday so the Cathedral was mute. Dr Atkinson had gone away, leaving what little had to be done in the hands of the deputy organist. Many of the canons had gone out of residence and even the Dean was visiting his son in London.

Mr Veal had his own deputies, and he allowed these assistant vergers more responsibility at these times, and himself more leisure.

'Mind you,' he said, leaning forward and tapping the table for emphasis, 'you can't give them too much responsibility. They're not ready for it. So I do my rounds, like always. I keep the keys.'

He nodded towards the table at the window. There was a big tray on it, and Mr Veal had laid out on it the keys that usually hung on the back of the cupboard door, together with a black notebook.

'Funny how keys wander,' he said. 'I make sure none of them have strayed. Redo the labels and check them off in my book. You can't afford to sleep on this job. There's a lot goes on here that most folk never realize.'

Neither of us said anything. It wasn't just the heaviness of the meal that kept us silent. In my case, at least, it was also the sense that I had no idea what I was going to do with the rest of the day. Food was, as always in my schooldays, a temporary distraction.

Perhaps Mr Veal sensed something of this. 'There's ratting up at Mr Witney's.'

I looked up. 'In his big barn?'

'Yes – all afternoon till the light goes.'

'We could go,' I said. 'He wouldn't mind, would he?'

'More the merrier. More than enough rats to go round.'

'Ratting?' Faraday said. 'I've never done that.'

'It's ripping fun,' I said.

'There are some sticks in my shed if you want them,'

38

Mr Veal said. 'Always best to take your own. You want one the right weight, don't you?'

Faraday was reluctant but he wasn't proof against my enthusiasm and Mr Veal's gentle encouragement. We found a couple of sticks and walked through the Porta. Angel Farm was across the green, beyond the theological college.

'Do we – do we actually hit them? The rats, I mean?'

'Of course we do.' I whacked the grass with my stick. 'But you have to be quick. Or the dogs get them first.'

'You've been ratting before?'

'Loads of times.' I had been ratting only once, in fact, with the vicar's son at home. 'It's awfully good sport – you'll see.'

We turned into the muddy drove to the farm. They had already started – I could hear the shouting and the excited barking. To tell the truth, I was a little nervous.

'Better put your cap in your pocket,' I said, taking mine off. 'You might lose it otherwise.'

My real reason was that our caps advertised the fact that we were King's School boys. The school was not universally popular in the town, and there was no point in courting trouble. Not that I was seriously worried. Mr Witney was a tenant of the Dean and Chapter, and the school subleased their playing field from him; he would keep an eye out for us.

Men and boys were milling around the yard. The barn doors were open, revealing a space large enough to take a laden wagon. Dogs were everywhere, small ones mainly, terriers and the like.

'That's like mine at home,' I said, pointing at a mongrel with a lot of spaniel in him. 'He's awfully bright – understands almost everything I say.'

This was a lie, as I did not have a dog. But I had pretended I had one for years. My aunt wouldn't let me have a real dog. It would bring mud into the house and, besides, who would look after it in term time? So I had a dog in my mind instead. The precise breed varied (he was often a mongrel) but his name was always Stanley, after a dog my father had owned when he was a boy. The dog's other permanent attributes included his almost human intelligence and his unswerving loyalty to me.

Mr Witney was concentrating his operations both inside and outside the barn. The building was very old, perhaps mediaeval in origin, and constructed of soft, crumbling sandstone. The target areas lay along the base of one of the immensely thick gable walls, both inside and out. Two or three men on each side were attacking the ground with spades, iron rods and pickaxes, breaking up the compacted earth. A score or so of men and boys gathered around the diggers, all of them armed with sticks. Dogs of all shapes and sizes scurried about everyone's legs, tails high in excitement.

Faraday and I sidled into the outskirts of the larger crowd, the one outside the barn. Nobody seemed to notice us. They were all staring at the diggers. Some of the dogs, careless of danger, were diving into the loosened soil and burrowing like maniacs with their front paws.

One of the dogs was already so far into the ground that only his hind legs and tail were visible. Suddenly he pulled himself out of the hole with a wriggling rat clamped between his jaws. He shook his prey in the air, and two other dogs instantly converged on him. One of them leapt up and grabbed the rat by its head. A tug of war ensued, each animal trying to wrest the rat from the other until the rat resolved the matter by dividing itself into two unequal parts.

I heard a sound beside me and glanced at Faraday. His face had gone white, the fleeing blood leaving a cluster of freckles scattered across the bridge of his nose and his cheeks.

'Come on,' I cried. 'It's—'

Another rat broke cover and darted to and fro among the sticks and stamping feet and snarling dogs. It saw an opening and shot towards the open field beyond. It was making for the gap between Faraday and me. People were shouting. I swung the stick down and felt the jar as it hit the ground, the impact running up my hands and arms.

'Well hit, young 'un!' shouted Mr Witney. 'That's the way.'

I looked down and saw to my surprise a little mass of bloodied fur, still squirming feebly.

'Oh God,' Faraday said.

A sort of frenzy seized me, a bloodlust. I ran berserk among the men and boys and the dogs and the rats. I held my stick in both hands and pounded it down, again and again. One of the dogs attached itself to me. How many rats did I kill or help to kill that day? Half a dozen, perhaps more?

Mr Witney put a stop to the ratting only when the light was beginning to fade.

It felt as if we had only been at the farm for five minutes but it must have been at least an hour and a half. The dog rubbed itself against my leg. It was a mangy little animal, a mongrel, with a piece of rope for a collar and a half-healed wound on its side.

'Well done, boy,' Mr Witney said. 'So you learn more than Latin and Greek at that school of yours.'

I bent down and scratched the dog between his ears. 'Good boy, Stanley,' I murmured. 'Good boy.' Just for a moment I was blindingly happy, dizzy with joy.

Faraday nudged my arm. 'Can we go back now? Please?'

I looked at his pale face and his big teeth, ghostly in the fading light, and all at once the joy evaporated.

'There's blood on you,' he said. 'There's blood everywhere.'

He was right. My hands were streaked with blood from the dog's muzzle and the handle of my stick. The corpses of rats lay everywhere, some complete, others in fragments. The dogs' interest in them diminished sharply once they stopped moving.

'Come on,' he said. 'Please.'

I glanced over my shoulder, hoping for a wave from Mr Witney or a nod of farewell from one of my comrades in the battle. But no one was looking at me. No one paid any attention when we left the yard and walked down the muddy lane towards the green.

For a few moments, for an hour even, I had been part of a group; I had played a useful part; I had been, in some small way, valued for what I did. That was all gone. Now I came to my senses and discovered that part of my collar had come adrift from my shirt and the tip of it was nudging my left ear. My overcoat was splashed with mud and cowpats, as well as blood. I had lost my cap. And I was alone once more with Faraday.

'They were talking about me,' he said in a voice that wobbled. 'Mr Nicholls was there. He knows.'

'Who's Nicholls?'

'He is a lay clerk. A tenor.' For a moment there was a hint of superiority in Faraday's voice. 'Not very good, though he thinks he is.'

The lay clerks were the basses and the tenors of the Cathedral choir. They were grown-ups. Many of them had been at the Choir School when they were young, and they still lived in the town.

'What does it matter if he recognized you?'

'You don't understand.' Faraday was always accusing me of that, and quite rightly. 'Mr Nicholls was pointing me out and whispering about me. They know.'

'I expect it was about your voice breaking and not being in the choir any more.'

'No. You should have seen their faces. They'd heard about . . . about the other thing.'

He meant the postal order. If Mr Nicholls knew about it, the story could no longer be confined to the Choir School and a handful of trusted outsiders like Mr Ratcliffe. It would be all over the place in a day or two, in the College and in the town.

'I can't bear it,' Faraday said.

I glanced at him and saw a tear rolling down his cheek.

'We'll go back to the Rat's now,' I said. 'We can make tea. If there's bread, perhaps we can have toast. He's got a toasting fork in the fireplace.'

'Thank you,' he said, blowing his nose. 'Thank you.'

7

Poor little devil. I was sorry for Rabbit. I wanted to help, as long as doing so wouldn't inconvenience me too much. The question is: did trying to help make matters worse?

It was starting to rain. In order to get back to the Sacrist's Lodging as swiftly as possible, I took us back through the Cathedral, which was not only shorter than going through the College or through the town but also, at that time of day, lessened the chance that we should meet anyone who knew either of us.

My suggestion wasn't entirely altruistic: if a boy from King's was found outside the College without his cap, it automatically earned him a beating. It was possible that the rule did not apply in the holidays, but I didn't want to put it to the test. Besides, I was starving, Mrs Veal's lunch a distant memory, and the idea of food was powerfully attractive.

Most people in the College used the Cathedral for shortcuts, and so did many townspeople. There were three doors open to the public – the west door under the great tower, the south door, which led through the ruins of the cloisters to the College, and the north door, from which a path led both to the High Street and to the Sacrist's

Lodging. Using the Cathedral also meant you kept dry. It was considered bad form to hurry, however.

We walked through the porch and pushed open the wicket in the west doors. It was dark, much darker, inside the Cathedral than it was outside. The lamps had not yet been lit, apart from one or two at the east end, beyond the choir screen.

The emptiness of the place enfolded us like a shroud. The air was cold and smelled faintly of earth, incense and candles.

Ahead and to the left, in the north aisle, was one of the great stoves, each surmounted by a black crown, that were supposed to keep the building warm. There was a faint but clearly audible chink as the coke shifted in its iron belly.

'I'm freezing,' Faraday said.

He walked over to the stove and held his hands to it.

'Hurry up,' I said. 'I'm starving.'

'Just a minute. I'm so cold.'

I joined him by the stove. If you stood about three inches away from it, you could actually feel the warmth of it on your skin. It wasn't so much that the stoves weren't occasionally hot: it was more that the Cathedral was eternally cold.

Faraday glanced at me. 'There's blood on your hands,' he said. 'And on your sleeve.' His voice lurched into a croak. 'It's everywhere.'

'Shut up,' I said. 'It doesn't matter. I can wash it off. What's water for?'

I turned my head to avoid seeing his white face and rabbit teeth. My eyes drifted away. It's a funny thing about buildings, how they take control of you and guide your eyes along their own lines, towards their own ends. In the Cathedral, the rhythm of columns and arches, diminishing in height as the layers climbed to the roof, made you look upwards and upwards. Towards heaven, the school chaplain once told us in a sermon. Or to the roof. Not that it matters in this case: the point is I looked up into the west tower.

Its west wall rises sheer, a cliff of stone pierced with openings: first the doors, then a great window which doesn't let in much light because of the stained glass. Then, higher still, bands of Norman arcading line the inside of the tower. The first set has a walkway that runs behind it. The next one, further up, is blind, its arches and pillars flattened against the tower wall behind. Above that still, 120 feet above the ground, is the painted tower ceiling, above which the tower rises, higher and higher, stage by stage, to the lantern that perches on top.

Sometimes one of the younger masters would take a party of boys up to the top as a treat. You went up a spiral staircase in the south-west corner, crossed the width of the tower by the walkway behind the lower arcade, climbed another set of stairs, and then another, until your legs felt twice as heavy as usual. Finally, you came to a wooden door that led on to the leads, more than two hundred feet from the ground.

Up there was another world, full of light, where a wind was always blowing. You felt weightless, as if floating in a balloon. Far below were the streets of the town and tiny, foreshortened people scurrying through the maze of their lives, oblivious of the watchers above. Beyond the town stretched the Fens as far as the eye could see, their flatness dotted with the occasional church tower or tree or house, which served to emphasize the monotony rather than relieve it; and at the circular horizon, the sky and the earth became one in a blue haze; and it no longer mattered which was which.

I had been up to the top of the west tower only once, about six months earlier before the end of the summer term. It had been a bright, clear day. There was a story, the master said, that a day like this you could see almost every church in the diocese from here. I tried to count the churches I could see. But I soon gave up and thought instead about Jesus in the wilderness, and how the devil took him up to a high place and tempted him.

If I had been Jesus, I would have struck a deal with the devil. In return for my soul, I wanted not to be at school; I wanted to live at home with my parents; and I wanted to have a dog called Stanley.

I remembered all that as I stood by the stove with my bloody hands. I was still thinking about it when I saw the man. He was walking from left to right, quite slowly, along the walkway behind the lower arcade, perhaps ninety feet above our heads. The light was so poor I couldn't see him clearly. When he passed behind one of the pillars he seemed to dissolve and then reconstitute himself on the other side.

'Can you hear it?' Faraday said.

Irritated, I glanced at him. 'What?'

'Those notes.'

'Shut up, Rabbit.'

I looked back at the arcade. The man wasn't there any more. It was conceivable he had put on a bit of speed and reached the archway at the northern end. Or he might have stopped behind a pillar. Or, and perhaps this was most likely of all, he hadn't been there in the first place. The Cathedral at dusk was full of indistinct shapes that shifted as you tried to look at them.

Faraday nudged me. 'There it is again.'

'What are you talking about?'

'The four notes I heard last night. Remember?' He hummed them, and they meant nothing to me. 'It's like the start of something.'

'You're potty,' I said. 'Come on, I want some toast.'

*   *   *

47

There was an odd sequel to this a few hours later, when we were having our evening meal at the Veals'.

While we ate, Mr Veal was in the parlour with us. He had begun to relax in our company, as we had in his.

'This place would fall apart at the seams without the Dean and me,' he said with obvious satisfaction. 'Some of these clerical gents would forget who their own mothers were. Heads in the clouds. And your masters aren't much better.'

I told him about the glorious ratting we had had at Angel Farm.

'So you missed the rain this afternoon?' he asked, for the minutiae of the weather's fluctuations fascinated him, as they did most grown-ups.

'Just about. It was beginning to spit as we were going back to Mr Ratcliffe's, so we cut up through the Cathedral.'

'We'll have worse tonight,' he said. 'Mrs Veal feels it in her bones. Her bones are never wrong.'

'I saw someone up the west tower,' I said.

'Up the west tower?' Mr Veal shook his head. 'Not at this time of year.'

'Well, I thought I saw someone.' I shrugged. 'But it was already getting dark. I could've been wrong.'

'No one was up there today,' Mr Veal said. 'There wouldn't be. You can take it as Gospel, young man. Not without me knowing.'

8

That evening Mr Ratcliffe made cocoa again. The three of us – four, if you counted Mordred – sat close to the fire.

The weather had changed during the afternoon. It was still cold, but clouds had rolled in from the south-west, bringing with it a wind that blew in gusts of varying strengths with lulls between them. The wind carried raindrops with it, and the promise of more to come. It rattled doors and windows in their frames. It sounded in the wide chimney.

It was Faraday who reminded Mr Ratcliffe about his promise.

'Please, sir – you said you'd tell us about Mr Goldsworthy.'

'Did I?'

'Yes, sir. You said there was a real story about the ghost.'

'Real? To be perfectly truthful, Faraday, I can't be absolutely sure which parts of the story are real and which are not. I don't think anyone can after all this time.'

'When did he live, sir?' I asked.

'Nearly two hundred years ago. He was the Master of Music, one of Dr Atkinson's predecessors. He was a composer, too. You remember the anthem we have on Christmas Day? The "Jubilate Deo"? He wrote that.'

Faraday's face was in shadow. But he shifted in his seat as if someone had touched him. It was the anthem that Hampson Minor had sung in Faraday's place.

'He died as a result of a fall,' Mr Ratcliffe went on, 'and he's buried in the north choir aisle. There's a tablet to him on the wall more or less opposite the organ loft.'

'But – why is he a ghost?' I said. Into my mind slipped an image of Dr Atkinson, who was small, red-faced and irascible, draped in a sheet and rattling chains like the Ghost of Christmas Past.

'*If* he is,' said Mr Ratcliffe. 'That's the question, isn't it?'

'Has anyone seen him, sir?' Faraday asked, leaning forward. 'They must have done. Otherwise, you wouldn't have said he was a ghost last night.'

'You must be patient.' Mr Ratcliffe began the elaborate ritual of cleaning, filling and lighting his pipe. 'Did you know that the Cathedral once had a ring of eight bells? One of our canons, Dr Bradshaw, wrote a standard treatise on the subject in the 1670s. *Campanologia Explicata*. There were eight bells, and they hung in the west tower. You know, I am sure, that our church bells are rung according to a series of mathematical permutations.' He looked up at us and took pity on our ignorance. 'It's like a pattern of numbers. Each bell has a number and it rings according to its place in the pattern.'

By now Mr Ratcliffe was crumbling flake tobacco into the palm of one hand. He fell silent, concentrating on rubbing the strands into a loose, evenly distributed mixture.

'Bells don't last for ever, you know. Our bells had to be taken down in the eighteenth century. They needed to be recast. This was done, at considerable expense. There was to be a service of dedication when the new ring of bells was rung for the first time. The Dean and Chapter asked Mr Goldsworthy to compose a special anthem to mark the occasion, to be based on Psalm one hundred and fifty. "Praise Him with the sound of the trumpet: praise Him upon the lute and harp".'

Mordred, who had been slumbering on Mr Ratcliffe's lap, jumped to the ground. He stretched himself out with luxurious abandon on the hearthrug.

'They say that Mr Goldsworthy was an ambitious man,' Mr Ratcliffe went on. 'And a troubled one. The Dean had a piece of patronage in his gift, the Deputy Surveyorship of the Fabric, a position that came with an income of two hundred pounds a year for the holder, and entailed no obligations apart from a few ceremonial duties. Mr Goldsworthy thought there was no reason why the post should not go to himself as to the next man. And the Dean gave him to understand that it might well be his, if his new anthem was a particularly fine piece of work that brought renown on the Cathedral. And, no doubt, on the Dean.'

As Mr Ratcliffe was speaking, Mordred rose to his feet. He stared at the three of us in turn and, to my surprise, came towards me and rubbed his furry body against me. I felt the vibration of his purring against my legs. Flattered by his attention, I bent down and stroked him.

'The problem was,' Mr Ratcliffe continued, 'Mr Goldsworthy found that for once his inspiration failed him. It couldn't have happened at a worse time. His career was at a crossroads. If he failed in the commission, he would earn the Dean's disfavour. To make matters worse,

I believe there was a lady in the case, and Mr Goldsworthy could not afford to marry without a larger income.'

The cat unsheathed the claws of his right paw and ran them into my calf. I squealed with pain and shock.

'Mordred!' Mr Ratcliffe said. 'I'm so sorry – he can be such an unmannerly animal. Perhaps one of you would put him outside.'

Mordred frustrated this design by going to ground under the grand piano, sheltered by the wall on one side and a pile of books on the other.

'What did he do then?' Faraday said. 'Did he compose the anthem in the end?'

'That's the strange part of it. It is said that he did. He told his friends that he had succeeded at the very last moment. He said the piece would be his masterpiece. The newly cast bells had already been hung in the tower. He found that if he went up into the tower himself, into the ringing chamber with pen and paper, the music came to him as if borne on the wind. But then came disaster.'

'He died?' I said, half hopefully, half fearfully.

Mr Ratcliffe held up a hand. 'Be patient, young man. No, the first thing to happen was that cracks were discovered in the tower, when the workmen were hanging the new bells. You see, the west tower was built in the Middle Ages. It simply wasn't designed for a ring of bells. It's not the weight of them, you know. It's the vibration they cause when they are rung. The Cathedral Surveyor told the Dean and Chapter that there could be no question of ringing the new ones.'

'Which is why there aren't any bells now,' I said.

'Yes – because they could well bring the tower crashing about everyone's ears. The Surveyor said that the new bells must come down, and the tower had to be strengthened as soon as possible, and braced with iron ties. The Dean raged against this – his reputation, his judgement, was at stake. But he was forced to give way in the end. So there was no longer a need for an anthem to celebrate the new bells, and no longer any purpose on wasting a perfectly good piece of patronage on the Master of Music.'

'What happened to it?' Faraday asked. 'The anthem, I mean.'

The anthem, I noticed, not the man: the Rabbit's as mad as a hatter; and I smiled at my own joke.

Mr Ratcliffe lit his pipe and tossed the match into the fire. 'No one knows for sure. Perhaps it was never written or perhaps it was destroyed. But the sad part is what happened to Mr Goldsworthy. The story was that he had left the manuscript in the west tower, where he had been working on it. One winter evening, he went up to retrieve it. But he was not aware that the workmen had already begun to remove the new bells from the tower. There are hatches in the floors at the various levels, to allow the bells to be lowered down from the belfry to the floor of the tower. By some mishap, the workmen had left open the hatch at the lowest stage, which is the ringing chamber just above the painted ceiling. There was very little light up there and poor Goldsworthy must have stumbled in the dark.'

The room was no longer cosy, despite the cups of cocoa and Mr Ratcliffe's tired, gentle voice. I glanced at him, sitting back in his chair. The old man looked back at me and, for an instant, by some trick of the firelight, he had Mordred's eyes in his face. Amber, flecked with green. But the cat was still lurking under the grand piano.

'He fell?' Faraday said, his voice awed.

'More than a hundred feet on to the floor of the tower.' Mr Ratcliffe had returned to normal. 'The poor fellow was killed outright.'

It occurred to me that five or six hours earlier I must

have walked across the very spot where Mr Goldsworthy's body had lain.

'It was an accident, of course,' Mr Ratcliffe said. 'That's what they decided. There was nothing to show it had been suicide, after all, and a verdict of accidental death meant that he could have a Christian burial.'

'Did someone look for the anthem?' Faraday asked.

I wondered why Rabbit was so concerned about a bit of music. What did it matter, after all, beside the fact of a man's death? But then I have never been able to understand the value that people place on music. It's nothing but a series of sounds, sounds without meaning.

'They searched his pockets. It wasn't there, though they did find a pen and a portable inkwell. They looked among his papers. They looked in the tower, as well. But they didn't find any trace of it. The anthem had vanished, if it had ever existed.'

'Perhaps it hadn't,' I said.

'The lady who was engaged to Mr Goldsworthy said that he had played her some of the melodies. She said it was a thing of ravishing beauty, that it would draw the heart out of an angel. But I suppose in the circumstances she would be inclined to have a high opinion of the piece.'

Mr Ratcliffe rose stiffly from his chair and knocked out his pipe. He looked down at us in our chairs.

'It's long past time for you boys to be in bed.'

'But, sir,' I protested. 'What about the ghost?' I could not help thinking of the person I had glimpsed in the west tower this afternoon. 'Do people see him? Does he haunt the tower?'

'Poor Goldsworthy?' Mr Ratcliffe shook his head. 'Not as far as I know. No, it's his music that people hear. Or they say they do. Fragments of melody, just a few notes.' He waved his pipe in the direction of the Cathedral. 'It's as if the anthem was broken into many pieces in the fall. And all the notes it contained were thrown up into the air. They are still there. Looking for each other. Trying to come together again.'

9

The next day, Friday, 27 December, was grey and blustery, with showers of rain that attacked from unexpected angles and worked their way through the crevices of one's clothing to the naked skin beneath.

I explained my problem about the lost cap to Mr Ratcliffe. He considered the matter gravely and gave it as his opinion that it would not be a beatable offence if I were caught outside the College without a school cap during the holidays. If I had any trouble, I was to refer the complainant to himself.

But I could not go out without a hat. That would not be seemly or indeed good for my health. He lent me one of his own, a battered, shapeless thing of tweed, with a trout fly fixed to the band. It was too large for my head and rested loosely on my ears. But it kept me decent, according to the standards of those days, and it kept me dry. It smelled powerfully of mothballs, with a hint of stale tobacco.

In the morning, Faraday and I went into town. He waited outside while I tried my luck with three tobacconists in turn. The first two refused to serve me but in the third, a little shop in an alley between the High Street and Market Street, I struck lucky. The proprietor had left the establishment in the temporary charge of his elderly mother, who was very shortsighted. I put on my gruffest voice when I asked for ten Woodbine cigarettes – unlike Faraday's, my voice had settled down to a sort of croak after the ups and downs of the previous year. That and Mr Ratcliffe's hat seemed to allay any suspicions the woman might have had.

Once outside, I showed Faraday my booty. He reacted with gratifying horror.

'If you're caught, they'll chuck you out,' he whispered.

'What does it matter?' I said grandly. 'I don't care.'

He glanced at me under the brim of his cap and I felt reproved by the misery in his eyes. By buying cigarettes I was merely toying with the risk of expulsion. It was improbable I would be caught smoking and doubly improbable that I would be expelled for doing it, particularly in the school holidays. But Faraday almost certainly faced expulsion already: and if by any chance he was allowed to stay at school, the alternative he faced was almost worse – years of persecution. In either case, I pictured the shame of the stolen postal order pursuing him through his blighted adult life until his miserable death.

In the meadows between the Cathedral and the river, there stood a steep, heavily wooded hill, which had once formed part of a castle made of earth and wood. It was as safe as anywhere to smoke. I scrambled up it, with Faraday trailing after me because he had nothing better to do and my company was better than his own.

At the top was a clearing of rough grass with a rotting summerhouse that stank of foxes. I stood on the remains of the verandah in front of it and smoked two Woodbines in swift succession. I tried my best to give the impression that I was enjoying an exquisite pleasure but in truth the cigarettes made me feel rather sick.

Meanwhile Faraday moved restlessly about the clearing.

As I was smoking the second cigarette, he came back to my side.

'I say,' he said. 'You know the anthem? The one that was lost?'

I squinted through the smoke at him. 'Yes.'

'It would be marvellous if it was found after all this time. Wouldn't it?'

I shrugged. 'I suppose so. For choirboys and chaps like that.'

'Just because it hasn't been found, it doesn't mean it isn't there.'

My mind filled with a picture of all those lost notes, black blobs with little tails and other attachments, floating in the air like dead leaves in a strong breeze.

'But where?' I said. 'I'm sure they looked everywhere.'

'I think it's in the tower,' Faraday said. 'I mean, that's where he was when he fell. He had his pen and ink with him, remember.'

'Don't be an ass. They must have searched especially hard up there.'

'But perhaps they didn't look hard enough. Look – just suppose we looked for it, and we found it. Wouldn't it be wonderful? They'd make an awfully big fuss. I shouldn't wonder if they put it in the newspapers. And we'd be – well, we'd be sort of heroes, wouldn't we?'

He stared expectantly at me, his mouth open, the rabbit teeth displayed.

My imagination was beginning to stir, even though the idea had come from Faraday. It would impress everyone at school no end if we found the anthem. I imagined the news filtering through to my aunt, miraculously restored to full health for the purpose, and even to my parents in India. I imagined their delight, their pride.

'What do you think?' he said.

'But we can't get up there.'

'I bet we could find a way. I've a plan.'

I was careful to preserve my dignity by not showing too much enthusiasm. 'There'd be a beastly stink if they catch us.'

'Not if we find it. They wouldn't mind what we'd done. They'd wipe the slate clean.'

I understood at last what Faraday meant, what his motive was. He thought that the lost anthem was his chance of salvation, perhaps his only one. If he found it, it would neutralize the disgrace of the postal order; it would make up for his broken voice and for no longer being head of the choir. The school would come back next term to find him a hero. And I would be a hero, too.

If he found it.

I dropped the cigarette butt and ground it into the wet earth with my heel. 'All right,' I said. 'At least it'll give us something to do.'

In my heart of hearts, I didn't believe that Faraday would do anything. It's easy enough to come up with these schemes but quite another to put them into practice.

He didn't mention the idea again for an hour or two. We went to the Veals' for lunch, our midday dinner. Afterwards I walked up to Angel Farm, followed by the reluctant Faraday, in case Mr Witney had decided on a second day of ratting. But the farmyard was deserted apart from a dog that barked furiously at us and made savage runs towards us to the limit of its chain.

'Let's go to the Cathedral,' he suggested.

I didn't say anything but we fell into step together and, as we had done the day before, walked through the long street leading from the green to the west door.

It was much earlier in the afternoon than it had been on our last visit. The Cathedral, even on this grey day, seemed brighter and more welcoming. I took this as a

59

good omen. We stood in the very centre of the space beneath the west tower and looked up at the painted ceiling.

More than a hundred feet high, Mr Ratcliffe had said.

'You can't see the trapdoor,' Faraday said, clearly disappointed.

I wondered what a fall from that height would do to a man. Would it compress him, ram his legs into his body and his head into his shoulders?

'What's the painting of?' I said.

Faraday stared upwards. 'I don't know. It looks like angels playing harps and things.'

He went over to a short flight of steps in the thickness of the wall, almost invisible because it was in the shadow of one of the great columns that supported the tower. At the top of the steps was a heavy door. This was where the stairs to the tower began.

I glanced over my shoulder. No one was in sight. I tried the door. It was locked. We stood and looked at it. The door was made of old, scarred oak with great iron hinges. The lock looked more modern, judging by the size of the keyhole, and smaller than I would have expected.

There was a clattering behind us as a small party of visitors burst through the west door. One of them had a guidebook in hand and was acting as tour leader.

None of them gave us a second glance, but we scurried away like a pair of startled animals.

10

I had underestimated Faraday, or perhaps underestimated the power of his desperation. When we went to the Veals' for tea that evening, Mr Veal was not at home. He had gone to visit an assistant verger who was in hospital after breaking his leg by falling off his bicycle.

'Never liked those bicycles,' Mrs Veal said. 'Nasty dangerous things. Against nature.'

She gave us scrambled eggs and filled us up afterwards with bread and dripping. It's strange how clearly I remember the food she gave us. I suppose it must be because we were so poorly fed in term time.

After we had finished, Faraday touched my arm. 'Take the plates out to her,' he whispered. 'Ask her how she makes her eggs like that.'

'What are you talking about?'

'Go on.' He gave me a little push. 'Ask her anything you like. Just keep her in the kitchen for a few minutes.'

I did as he told me, though it seemed quite wrong that Faraday should be giving me instructions. I didn't need to ask Mrs Veal about her scrambled eggs. She was already washing up so I dried the plates and cutlery for her, and she asked me about my aunt in hospital and my parents in India. She was a kind woman, kinder than we deserved.

When I returned to the parlour, Faraday was sitting by the lamp and reading, or pretending to read, the local paper, which Mr Veal had left on the arm of a chair. He looked up as I entered and gave me a small, sly smile.

We walked back to the Sacrist's Lodging through the College.

'I've got the key,' he said. 'It says "West Tower Stair" on it.'

'Won't Veal notice?'

'I don't think so. There's two other ones there on the same hook. This is one of the spares.'

We walked in silence for a moment. Faraday was probably right. The verger had finished his inventory of the keys, so he would have no need to look closely at them. Besides, the Cathedral was now locked up for the night.

I was suddenly struck by such an obvious and insuperable objection that I laughed out loud – partly, I suspect, from relief.

'What is it?' Faraday said, staring down and looking at me.

'It's all very well, us having the key to the stairs,' I said. 'But the Cathedral's locked up at night. And we can't go up in daytime. Someone would see us for sure.'

He gave a snicker of laughter. 'Don't worry about that. I can get in the Cathedral whenever I want. We can go tonight.'

I nearly kicked him. The smug little Rabbit.

We passed an interminable evening with Mr Ratcliffe, the three us reading by the fire. I was bored. Living with Mr Ratcliffe was turning me into an old man like him, a creature of habit. On the other hand, part of me wanted this time by the fire to last for ever. Part of me wanted to be bored.

Mordred disgraced himself again. He brought in another mouse, which he played with, despite our attempts to stop him, and then allowed it to escape for the time being into the relatively safe haven of the floor beneath the piano. During the struggle, he scratched my hand, drawing blood. Finally he went to sleep on the hearthrug with the air of a job well done.

'I'm so sorry he injured you again,' Mr Ratcliffe said. 'He's quite unteachable, I'm afraid, and I suspect he doesn't have a very nice nature to begin with.'

'Why do you keep him then, sir?' Faraday asked.

'One must try to make the best of animals, don't you think? And of people, for that matter. He's a farm cat by breeding, you see. Mrs Thing's sister is married to a farmer, and I believe he came from there . . . But farm cats never truly adjust to living in houses. They never quite lose their wildness.'

At last it was time for bed. The sky was still cloudy but the rain had gone, and most of the wind. It was colder.

'We'll have snow before long, I shouldn't wonder,' Mr Ratcliffe said.

Faraday nudged me behind Mr Ratcliffe's back. This time I kicked him. I was growing tired of his nudges.

Mordred rose and stretched. He stalked out of the sitting room and sat by the front door, where he miaowed like a rusty hinge.

'Let him out, would you?' Mr Ratcliffe said.

I opened the door. Mordred slunk outside and disappeared into the darkness.

'Where does he go at night, sir?' I asked.

'Mordred? Heaven knows. Best not to enquire.'

'He can't stay outside all night, can he? Not in this weather.'

'I'm sure he manages quite well.' Mr Ratcliffe locked up and hung the key on the hook beside the front door. 'He's not an animal to go without his creature comforts.'

In our bedroom, I began to undress.

'Don't take too much off,' Faraday hissed. 'There's no point. It'll probably be freezing.'

'I'm tired. Let's do it tomorrow.'

'No, it's got to be tonight. We need to get the key back tomorrow. Besides, it's going to snow. If we wait till after that, we'll leave tracks.'

I shrugged. 'This is stupid.'

'I know what it is,' Faraday said. 'You're yellow.'

'I'm not yellow.'

'Yes, you are.'

We glared at each other across the room.

'Well,' he said. 'It's easy enough to prove it, isn't it?'

I said nothing. But I put on my pyjamas over my underclothes.

He was still watching me. His face was flushed. 'We'll have to wait until Ratty's in bed and fast asleep.'

'It'll be hours.'

'I don't care. I'll stay awake.'

We got into bed. I didn't bother reading. I turned on my side, away from Faraday, and closed my eyes. I knew I wouldn't sleep. I was too angry. Too afraid. So I sent up a prayer to my provisional God, promising to believe in Him for the rest of my life if He made Faraday fall asleep at once and stay asleep until morning.

11

Later, much later, I was wrenched from a deep sleep. Faraday was standing over me. He hadn't lit the gas but a candle was burning on the mantelpiece, sending shadows flickering across the room.

'Go away,' I said and shut my eyes again.

'Come on,' he whispered. 'It's time.'

He pulled back the covers and cold air washed over me. I sat up abruptly and pushed him away.

'You're crazy,' I said. 'Mad as a coot.' I tried to pull the covers back over me.

'You're yellow,' he said. 'Yellow.'

I swore at him and swung my legs out of bed. The bed creaked.

'Don't make a noise,' he said.

'Shut up, you ape. Bloody Rabbit. Go to hell.'

I pulled on the rest of my clothes, fumbling interminably with the buttons. Faraday opened the door. Carrying our shoes, we tiptoed out of the room and down the stairs. At every step we paused to listen for sounds from Mr Ratcliffe's bedroom.

We reached the hall without mishap and put on our shoes, hats and coats. We took it in turns to shield the candle flame, for light can betray you as much as noise.

By now I was fully awake. It would be too much to say that I was entering into the spirit of the thing, but taking second place to Faraday was beginning to irk me. I pushed him aside when he was about to lift the key from its hook. I was the one who unlocked the door and lifted the heavy latch. It made much less noise than I had expected. We slipped outside and closed the door behind us.

There were still clouds, though fewer and wispier than before and moving rapidly across the sky. The stars shone down between them.

We crossed the yard in front of the Sacrist's Lodging and let ourselves out through the gate in the wall. The lawn that bordered the east end of the Cathedral was covered in frost. Two of the lamps that burned all night stood at this end of the College – one nearby, at the gate leading to the north door, the other on the far side of the lawn. Yellow coronas of moisture hung around their lamps.

'We had better walk across the grass,' Faraday whispered in my ear. 'Quieter.'

We tiptoed across the gravel path and set off across the lawn in the direction of the further light.

'Where the devil are we going?' I said. 'How are we supposed to get inside?'

He ignored me. He ploughed on, head down against the cold wind. I plodded after him.

'God, it's freezing,' I whispered.

'I feel boiling. Come on.'

Faraday led us right round the east end of the church and down to the flagged path leading to the south door. I glanced back. Our ragged footprints marched across the frosty grass. We were now in the larger, grander part of the College, where the houses of the Dean and Chapter were.

I looked about us. All the windows I could see were in darkness. But there were more lamps here, stretching down the road leading to the Porta and the Veals' house.

Faraday made for the south door.

I hurried after him. 'What are you doing? It'll be locked.'

He took no notice but led the way into the south porch. This had been formed by an accident of history from the one surviving fragment of the east walk of the mediaeval cloister.

It was darker here, but Faraday did not slacken his pace. I blundered after him. He stopped abruptly just before the door into the Cathedral and I bumped into him.

He didn't try to open the door. Instead, he moved to the left. There was another door here, much smaller, set in a square-headed archway. He reached up, as high as he could, and ran his fingertips along the top of the lintel, palpating the stone. I heard a faint chink. A key turned in the lock. The door scraped open and a current of cool air smelling of candles swept out to meet us.

Faraday took my arm and drew me after him through the doorway. It was much darker here, an enclosed space. Faraday closed the door behind us.

'Where are we?' I whispered.

'The choir vestry.'

'But the door for that's in the nave.'

He laughed, showing his knowledge. 'This is the other door, the one Dr Atkinson uses when he needs to come in at night, or early in the morning, when the Cathedral's locked. He sent me to fetch something once. He said it could be useful for the head of the choir to know where to find the key.'

'You're not head of the choir now,' I said, too scared to be kind. 'You're not even in the choir.'

Faraday lit a match. We were in a long room with a central aisle across which benches faced each other. There was a grand piano at the far end, with a dozen or so music stands huddled together like a herd of skeletal creatures. This was where the choir practised.

Before the flame had died, Faraday had reached a cupboard and opened its door. He asked me to light and hold up another match.

'We mustn't risk the gas,' he said. 'But there are some candles here.'

Most of the shelves held books of music. But the top shelf was filled with a jumble of objects, through which Faraday rummaged while I lit match after match. He unearthed three candle stumps, a candle lantern and another box of matches. He lit one of them, put it in the lantern and closed the glass. A faint radiance spread through the vestry. It made me feel better. It made what we were doing seem less strange.

Holding up the lantern, Faraday opened a desk that stood at the far end of the room. In a moment he gave a cry of triumph and held up a long key.

'What's that for?'

'The door from the choir vestry to the Cathedral.'

'All these keys without labels,' I said. 'Old Veal would have a fit if he knew.'

We snorted with suppressed laughter, the tension forcing its way out as a bubble of mirth.

'Atky doesn't let him in here,' Faraday said. 'They hate each other.'

He unlocked the door into the Cathedral. This was nine feet tall beneath a pointed archway; I had often seen the choir marching through it, two by two, processing into the Cathedral in their cassocks and surplices.

We passed into the south aisle. Faraday pulled the door to behind us but did not latch it.

For a moment we stood still, shocked by the immense, cold darkness around us. We were in the belly of a huge and unimaginably heavy stone beast. I had been scared before – but what I felt now was something different – terror, yes, but there was an element of awe mixed in with it. At night, the Cathedral lost its familiarity and became alien.

'Oh God.' Faraday sounded close to tears. 'It's horrible.'

'It's all right,' I said. 'It's just dark, that's all. You're not scared, are you?'

It was bravado that made me say that, together with the desire to contradict and needle Faraday. The more signs of fear he showed, the more my bravado increased.

'Come on, Rabbit. We haven't got all night.'

We set off down to the south aisle, which would take us the length of the nave to the west tower. At first we walked slowly, and then more quickly. I tried to suppress the idea that there might be someone behind us.

I glanced upward. I could not even see the vault of the aisle. On our right were the massive pillars of the nave, looming palely like a line of great grey oak trees. The lantern cast a puddle of light on the ground, enough to see where we were going, but little else.

Faraday touched my arm. 'We had better stay together.' I felt his hand sliding around my elbow and gripping it. 'If – if we hold on to each other, we can't get lost.'

He spoke in a whisper. All the time we were in the Cathedral that night, we spoke in whispers – except, of course, at the end. I felt there was a danger that we might be overheard: that someone or something was listening.

12

For me, the worst thing at that point was not the darkness but the sound of our footsteps on the flagstones. Try as we might, we could not walk quietly. Our steps sounded louder than usual, but muffled and dead, as if sinking into cotton wool.

At the end of the aisle we came to the south-west transept and the west tower. Our footsteps changed as they entered these wider, taller spaces. They sharpened and acquired an echo.

Faraday's grip tightened. 'Did you hear that? Someone's behind us.'

'Don't talk rot. You're getting windy. Let's go and look for your beastly anthem.'

Clinging to each other, we crossed to the door leading to the tower stairs. Faraday let go of me while he fumbled for the key he had borrowed from Mr Veal. I had privately cherished the hope that it would turn out to be the wrong key. But it turned sweetly in the lock.

The door opened outwards. We pulled it to its full extent, so it grated against the wall. The light from the lantern showed only the first two or three steps, spiralling in a clockwise direction into the utter blackness above.

We climbed, side by side, for the staircase at the lower level was wide enough for this. The air became colder and colder. After the vastness of the nave, the enclosed space pressed in on us. I was soon out of breath – from the climb and from fear. So was Faraday. Our laboured breathing was deafening. I wanted to put my hands over my ears.

I tried to count the steps as a distraction. We had been told that the west tower had nearly three hundred of them. But I lost my concentration somewhere in the forties. Then it was just ourselves with no distractions: our footsteps, our breathing and the light from our lantern sliding ahead into the darkness.

Faraday's breathing became irregular. He sniffed. Once or twice he gave an audible sob which he tried to disguise with a cough. He was crying. I pretended to ignore it.

I felt dizzy. I kept staggering against the outer wall of the staircase. It felt increasingly unnatural to be turning only in one direction and my body was making futile attempts to correct the situation.

We came at last to a small landing with a door set in the wall. There was no lock, only a latch. I lifted it and pulled the door open. I felt a current of air on my face.

'What's that?' Faraday said suddenly.

'What?'

'I thought I saw something. Over there.' He pointed over my shoulder, through the archway. 'A – sort of shadow.'

'That's just what it was,' I said. 'Stop being so jumpy.'

I stepped through the archway. We were on the walkway that ran behind the arcade across the west wall. Faraday held up the lantern. The arcading stretched away from us to the right; a miniature, almost domesticated version of the great pillars and arches that marched up either side of the nave.

Automatically my hand felt for the iron railing that ran between the pillars of the arcade. There was no other barrier between us and a drop of ninety-odd feet to the floor of the tower. It was a thin iron rod, cold and rough to the touch.

'It's too narrow,' Faraday wailed. 'We can't go side by side.'

'Give me the lantern. Hold on to the belt of my coat.'

In the daytime, when I had been taken up here with my classmates, this passage had been exciting, with its views into the tower and the body of the church right up to the huge east window beyond the choir. We had laughed at the squashed figures moving below and made jokes about dropping things on them.

By night, the passage was terrifying. I was standing on the edge of the world and the slightest misstep could send me tumbling away into the darkness.

I made myself let go of the rail. I focused my eyes on the light on the floor of the walkway, on the line on the left where it met the tower wall. I marched forward at a slow but steady pace, towing Faraday behind me.

On the far side, there was an archway. I passed beneath it and slumped against the wall. I felt the cold, rough stone against my cheek. I was trembling. I felt sick. I felt triumphant.

We were at the foot of another flight of steps, narrower than the first.

'Nearly there,' I said. My voice sounded like a stranger's.

We began to climb. Faraday stayed behind me, holding my belt. I reassured myself with the thought of all the people who must have climbed the stairs and walked across the arcade above the tower – the bell-ringers, the workmen, the tourists: hundreds of them, at least, if not thousands over the eight centuries this tower had stood here. It hadn't harmed them, and they had all come safely back to the ground. So why should it harm us?

But something had harmed Mr Goldsworthy.

This staircase was much shorter than the first, for the arcade was not far below the tower's painted ceiling. We came to another little landing, this one with a door. There was also a third, even narrower spiral staircase that continued the ascent of the tower. But we were going no higher.

I opened the door. As I did so, something touched my ankles. I glanced down, but nothing was there. I thought I would have heard a rat on these hard surfaces. And would a rat climb this high without the lure of food? The touch had been so light it could have been a draught of air.

'Is this it?' Faraday said. 'Are we here?'

'Yes,' I said. 'This is what you wanted, the place where they used to ring the bells.'

'Where Mr Goldsworthy fell from.'

'I tell you one thing, Rabbit: I'm not going any higher.'

'All right. It's here somewhere. I'm sure.'

'For God's sake, be careful.'

We advanced slowly into the ringing chamber. In daylight, it was bright enough – there were great windows on all four sides. It occupied the entire internal area of the tower. I looked up, remembering from my last visit a floor of huge, roughly trimmed planks on the network of beams. I couldn't see anything at all above our heads. A sense of futility washed over me.

'You won't find anything here,' I said. 'This is stupid. It would have been better to come in daytime, if you had to come at all.'

'It's not stupid. Anyway, we agreed – we'd have been seen if we'd come in the day.'

'Well, you're here now. Hurry up and find it.'

'We can search with the lantern. Maybe . . . maybe there's a loose stone or a board that lifts up or—'

'And maybe pigs fly,' I interrupted. 'You can look if you want. I'm staying here. But don't take long or I'll leave without you. And I'll leave you in the dark.'

Faraday took the lantern from me and held it up. All it did was emphasize how much darkness there was. He looked so forlorn, holding up the lantern, so pathetic, like one of those sentimental engravings my aunt had in her drawing room with titles like *His Father's Son* or *The Light of the World*.

He went down on his hands and knees and crawled slowly across the room, examining each board. He was such a ridiculous sight, a black blob on all fours, an enormous nocturnal insect. I wanted to laugh. I wanted to cry. Most of all, I wanted to escape from the Cathedral, go back to the Sacrist's Lodging, crawl into bed and pull the covers over my head.

Suddenly, Faraday raised his hand. 'Did you hear it?' He was so excited he forgot to whisper. 'And there it is again.'

I thought he had gone mad. 'What?'

'Those notes – the music I heard. Those four notes.' He sang them to me in his pure treble voice: 'La-la-la-la.'

'I can't hear it.'

'Shh – there's more. Listen.'

He tried to sing the new notes but this time his voice betrayed him. He croaked like a frog. Not that it mattered one way or another to me because the la-la-la-la was just noise as far as I was concerned.

Anyway, I didn't believe him, not really.

'There's something here,' he said in a different voice, excited and breathless. 'I think it's moving. Yes, it is. It's showing me where to look.'

I couldn't see what he was doing because his body was

in the way. 'Rabbit! For God's sake, come back! You must be near that trapdoor if you're not on it already.'

I had a sickening vision of the trapdoor breaking free, Faraday falling, just like Goldsworthy, to the floor of the tower below.

At that moment, the lantern went out.

13

'I'm scared,' Faraday said. 'I'm so scared.'

In the darkness his voice seemed to come from very far away. I had not realized what a difference that little lantern made.

'It's all right,' I said, though it felt all wrong. 'Find the other candles. Light one of those.'

I heard a scrabbling sound. Then silence. Then ragged breathing and more scrabbling.

'Hurry up,' I said. 'Come on, Rabbit, we haven't got all night.'

'I . . . I can't find them.' He sounded further away than he had been.

'Don't be stupid.' I heard the panic in my voice. I swallowed it. 'The ones from the choir vestry. Remember?'

'I put them down when I was looking for the key. I must have forgotten to pick them up.'

I bit my lower lip and tasted blood. 'We haven't time for jokes.'

'It isn't a joke. I'm sorry.'

I nearly shouted at him. But I knew there was no point. 'You've got matches,' I said. 'Light one and find where I am. Walk towards me. When the match goes out, I'll say something. Come towards the sound.'

There was another delay. Then a scrape and a flare of light, shocking in its intensity.

'It's the last one,' he said.

Faraday rose to his feet as he spoke. He was in the centre of the ringing chamber, I saw, which might well be the very place where the trapdoor was. He moved too quickly. The flame guttered and died.

For the first time we were in complete darkness. I felt dizzy again. The tower sensed our new weakness. It seemed to shift beneath my feet like a sleeping giant making a minute adjustment to its position.

Faraday whimpered.

'Come towards me,' I whispered. 'Keep together.'

I heard him crawling. A moment later the sound stopped.

'Hurry up,' I hissed.

'I can hear it.'

'What?'

'The music.'

'For God's sake – shut up about that damned music. Come here.'

'It's beautiful,' he murmured. But he started to crawl again.

I turned round, stretched out my hands and tried to find the door. I knew it wasn't far away. But the darkness had disorientated me. Faraday was still shuffling towards me.

'Where are you?' he said. 'Where are you?'

'Here, you fool.'

He sounded much nearer than I had expected. Something brushed the skirt of my coat. I jumped back and screamed like a girl. Something rattled in my coat.

'It's me,' Faraday said. 'Oh, I'm so glad we're together.'

So was I, though I didn't say so.

'What was that?' he said. 'When I touched you . . . it sounded like—'

'Matches,' I said. 'Matches.'

I fumbled in the pocket of my overcoat. Hours ago, in another lifetime, I had stood on top of the little wooded hill with Faraday and smoked two Woodbines. Afterwards, I had hidden both the cigarettes and the matches in my coat. I had a hole in one of the pockets, which made it possible to push contraband items deep into the lining.

My fingers were cold and shaking. The hole in the pocket was small. It took me an age to find and extract the matches. I shook the box. It sounded hollow, nearly empty.

I opened it, first making sure it was the right way up, and counted the remaining matches. There were only six left.

'I can still hear it,' Faraday said. 'The music.'

'Shut up. If we're careful we can just do it.' I calculated that we would have to use the matches only when we really needed them; for most of the time we would have to rely on our sense of touch. 'Hold on to my belt again.'

He obeyed. I scraped the first match on the side of the box. It misfired, the head crumbling to nothing.

'Are they damp?' Faraday said.

I didn't reply. That was what I was afraid of. I tried again: this time the match fired up. I turned. The door was on my right, perhaps three yards away. I took a step towards it. The movement made the flame flicker and die.

My fingers brushed against the wood of the door.

'Light another match,' Faraday said.

'Not yet. Just follow me. We'll go down the stairs very slowly. Don't hurry. Keep your right hand on the wall.'

Faraday was so close to me I felt his breath on my neck. The stairs were steep. I concentrated on the wall, on finding the rise of each stair with my foot, on keeping Faraday from going too quickly.

The archway leading from the landing to the arcade was just visible ahead of us. I reached the landing and stopped. Faraday bumped into me. I took out the box of matches. Just as I was poised to light one, he said, 'It's not quite dark.'

I ignored him. I thought that, after the confined space of the ringing chamber and stairs, it was naturally a little less dark in the body of the Cathedral.

I struck the third match. The flame burst out, dazzling me. Beyond the archway was the passageway behind the arcade and, at the end, the open door to the next staircase. All we had to do was keep to the wall on our right and not think about what lay on our left.

'Boys?' a man shouted far below. 'Boys?'

Faraday said something I couldn't catch. I held on to the pillar of the arch and looked down into the church. Light was moving in the nave.

'Boys! Where are you?'

It was Mr Ratcliffe. His voice sounded younger and more vigorous than usual, but very far away.

'Up here, sir,' I called. 'In the west tower.'

I heard his hurrying footsteps. He came out of the south aisle and into the nave. He tried to run but couldn't manage it. He slowed to a fast walk. He was carrying a lantern, which swung wildly to and fro in his hand.

Mr Ratcliffe reached the space under the tower. He stood panting in a puddle of light.

'I can't see you,' he called. 'Where are you?'

I struck a match.

'Good God – you idiotic children! Stay where you are. Don't move an inch.'

It was a relief to be told what to do. Mr Ratcliffe's footsteps hurried across the floor. The sound changed as he mounted the staircase but we could still see him.

'We never found it,' Faraday said. 'The anthem, I mean.'

'If you don't shut up about that bloody anthem, I'll bloody kill you,' I hissed.

He started to cry, irritating little sniffles. It enraged me that he could be such a self-centred beast. I was about to be in the worst trouble I had ever been in and it was his fault. I saw now what I should have seen earlier: that being caught didn't matter to him, because he was already in disgrace. But it was different for me.

The footsteps were nearer now. I heard Mr Ratcliffe's laboured breathing. Light glowed at the far end of the arcade, growing stronger every minute.

There he was, in the doorway, gasping for air, holding the lantern high.

'Don't – move—' he said again, sucking in breath between words.

It was Mr Ratcliffe but it did not look like him. He had taken his teeth out for the night, and his face had collapsed in on itself, making him a stranger with a familiar voice.

'I – I shall come over – to you. Bring you back – one by one.'

He was hatless, his hair unbrushed. He wore his over-coat, which hung open, revealing a dressing gown and striped pyjamas.

'Don't move,' he repeated yet again. 'Please. Please.'

He edged on to the passageway and staggered slowly towards us. 'Don't move,' he muttered. 'Don't move.'

'Look,' Faraday said loudly and urgently. 'Look—'

Mr Ratcliffe's head jerked to the right. His body twisted after it. He fell heavily against the railing. There was a moment when nothing happened, when everything simply stopped moving. Then the railing gave way.

The lantern clattered to the floor of the passage. The candle guttered but the flame lasted another second or two.

Time enough and more for Mr Ratcliffe to fall into the darkness.

14

Faraday wouldn't move. He sat down on the bottom step and started to cry. I left him to it. I crawled across the arcade – it seemed safer that way. I found the lantern. The glass was broken but the candle was there.

Once I was safely at the other end of the walkway, I lit the stub, which was still warm. It took me several minutes because my hands were shaking so much, and I wasted two more matches, including the last one.

When the candle was alight, I called out, 'Sir? Sir? Can you hear me?' I knew it was stupid, but I did it all the same. 'Sir? Are you all right?'

'He won't hear,' Faraday said. 'He can't hear.'

I looked back at him. He was still sitting on the bottom step.

'Come across,' I said.

'I can't. I'll fall. My legs are shaking. My head hurts.'

'You've got to. Come on, Rabbit. I'll come over and fetch you.'

'No,' he said. 'I won't. I won't let you. You'll make me fall.'

'Don't be stupid.'

'You can't make me.'

I didn't want to leave Faraday behind, for my sake as

much as his. But I had to find out what had happened to Mr Ratcliffe. I had to fetch help.

I went down the spiral staircase. It was relatively easy going after what had gone before, for the steps were wide and shallow. I forced myself not to hurry.

At the bottom, I cupped the flame with my free hand and moved slowly towards the west door. Mr Ratcliffe lay, a darker shadow than the rest, about a yard away from it. He was on his back. The overcoat had spread around him like a pair of black wings.

I put the candle carefully on the ground beside him. 'Sir,' I said. 'Sir – please wake up.'

I knew he was dead. I had known all along. But I touched him. It seemed important to do that, a sign of respect, of sorrow. I felt the stubble on his cheek. I tried to put his overcoat over him: to keep him warm, perhaps, or to make him decent.

I looked up, into the darkness. 'Faraday? Can you hear me?'

'Yes.'

'I'm going for help. Just stay where you are.'

I picked up the lantern. There was a savage draught by the door and the candle had no glass to protect it. The flame died as if a pair of fingers had snuffed it.

'I say . . .' Faraday's voice drifted down to me. 'I can hear it again. The music.'

I have no idea how long it took me to escape from the Cathedral. I wandered in the dark, in the belly of the stone beast. More by luck than good judgement I found the south nave aisle. I knew I was there because I could feel the shape of the memorial tablets that lined its wall.

From then it was simply a matter of working my way up to the choir vestry. I went through the vestry and tugged open the door to the south porch.

There was a little light here, for one of the College lampposts was fifty yards away on the road to the Porta. I walked through the porch. I glanced to my left. Our footprints were still visible on the grass. That was how Mr Ratcliffe had known we were in the Cathedral.

Something touched my leg below the knee.

I looked down. A cat walked briskly but without haste through the archway of the porch and slipped through the bars of the gate leading to the Deanery garden.

Was it Mordred? It seems far-fetched to think it might have been. But cats are strange animals, and he was a stranger cat than most. I remember that touch on my ankle as we were climbing the first staircase of the tower.

I fled through the College to the Veals' house. I have a vivid memory of hammering on their door, of screaming and crying until Mr Veal came down in his dressing gown, carrying a poker.

Later I remember hot, sweet tea in the kitchen. Mr Veal wasn't there – I suppose he must have gone to the Cathedral. But Mrs Veal bustled about in a dressing gown, with a cap on her head. It was she who saw that my hands were bloody, and so was the sleeve of my coat.

But that can't be right, I thought. My hands can't be bloody now. They had been bloody on Boxing Day, after the ratting at Angel Farm.

I think the doctor came. I think I was given a sleeping draught and put to bed in a little room beside the Veals' bedroom.

There's not much more to tell. I spent the next few days at the Veals' house. I slept and ate a great deal. I answered questions, often the same ones, over and over again. The Veals asked the questions first. Then the headmaster, a remote figure who had never condescended to speak to me before, then the doctor again. Then two police officers, one after the other, and a man in a suit with a gold watch chain, who I think was perhaps a solicitor.

I didn't ask about Faraday but the headmaster told me anyway. Mr Veal had brought him down from the tower. He was running a high fever and he had been taken to the cottage hospital.

His illness, I heard later, was diagnosed as brain fever, a convenient term in those days that covered a multitude of conditions. I don't know what a doctor would have called it now. Faraday recovered, I heard later, and his guardian sent him abroad to convalesce in one of the German spa towns.

My aunt was still in hospital herself, though she was well enough to return home by the middle of January. There must have been frenzied discussions about what on earth to do with me in the meantime. In the end, the school persuaded the vicar of my aunt's village to take me in until she was able to cope with me again.

Mr Ratcliffe, I presume, was buried, and his house was given to strangers. I don't know what happened to Mordred.

In one way, everything turned out well – at least for me. I didn't have to go back to school. The vicar and his family were kind, and all my Christmas presents were waiting for me there.

Better still, when my aunt came home and I moved back to live with her, she decided I could have a puppy. I called him Rusty, not Stanley. For a month or two I had lessons with the vicar for four mornings a week. Then my aunt sent me as a dayboy to the grammar school in the nearest town. I was quite happy there, once I had grown used to it, though I never made any close friends.

So you might say that I had everything I wanted. But somehow it turned out to be not quite what I wanted after all.

*　　*　　*

I never went back. What would have been the point? My parents came home a year later. When we met again, they didn't talk about what happened and nor did I, though once, years later, my mother made some reference to my stay at the vicarage – 'after you were ill'.

But I wasn't ill. It was Faraday who was ill, not me.

I never saw Faraday again, though there was a time in the 1920s when I wished I could have talked to him about all this: he would have been the one person who might have understood, who might have known more. But Faraday went missing in action at the Third Battle of Ypres in September 1917. His body was never found.

I am quite aware that everything that happened that night is explicable in a perfectly straightforward way. Two silly schoolboys went into the Cathedral by night for a prank and climbed part of the way up the west tower before compounding their folly by plunging themselves into darkness. The elderly gentleman whose hospitality they had abused came to rescue them. He was not in the best of health. Climbing the tower stairs in a state of acute anxiety brought on a heart attack, which led him to fall – though the doctor was not able to tell whether it was the heart attack or the fall that actually killed him. The younger boy was running a fever at the time, which may have been some excuse for his irresponsible behaviour. But there was no excuse for the behaviour of the older boy.

All this is true. But it leaves out so much. We went up the west tower because of the story of Mr Goldsworthy: because of his anthem for the bells that were never rung, and because of his dying fall from the ringing chamber.

La-la-la-la. We went up the tower because of lost notes that only Faraday heard.

Was Mordred in the Cathedral that night? Was it he who brushed against me on the tower stairs and left the south porch when I did? Did Faraday see something when we were climbing the stairs and, later, just before Mr Ratcliffe had his seizure? After the ratting at Angel Farm, did I really glimpse a man in the arcade passageway when we came through the Cathedral?

Finally, can I trust my own memory?

La-la-la-la.

Lost notes and broken melodies. Sometimes, when I wake up suddenly, I am full of happiness. I know that I have heard in a dream I can no longer remember those notes that Faraday heard and tried to sing to me in his cracked voice. But I don't understand music. And I never remember my dreams.

THE LEPER HOUSE

1

Somewhere along the way, Mary mislaid her religion. The funeral was a humanist affair in a chapel, or whatever they call it, attached to a crematorium. There must have been nearly two hundred mourners. She had been only thirty-eight when she died, which is why her death touched so many lives – and why there was a sense of outrage in the air, rather than resignation.

Alan himself acted as master of ceremonies. He was used to public speaking and chairing meetings – he was the headmaster of a school about fifteen miles from Norwich. He kept his emotions as firmly in check as the timing.

'How brave,' whispered one of my neighbours.

'He's bearing up wonderfully,' said a friend. 'Especially when you think—'

'He has to be brave for the children.'

The friend nodded. 'At least her poor parents are dead.'

The coffin was at the end of the room. It was one of those environmentally friendly ones, designed to make a posthumous statement of faith in the possibility of a greener world to come, as it slid towards its complete destruction in the furnace. It had nothing to do with the

Mary I remembered most vividly: the sideways glances, the grazed knees and the shrill giggles.

Alan took us through Mary's life at a brisk pace – we had a time slot at the crematorium, and death waits for no one. He described our parents – a nurse and an estate agent, respectively – and the loving upbringing they had given her. He talked about her pet rabbit, Matilda, and our old dog, who recognized her step even when he was old and blind. (Alan did not mention the dog's incontinence and appallingly bad breath.) He talked about their meeting at university, the rocky road of their romance and the happy years of their marriage. He waxed lyrical about the dedication she had brought to her career as a primary teacher and the devotion her pupils gave her in return. Finally, by way of peroration, he talked of their children, Matthew and Alice, as the crowning joys of her life.

The children were sitting in the front row. I had caught a glimpse of them as they came in. They both looked like Alan, poor kids, all long nose and small chin; there was not a trace of Mary. Maybe that was no bad thing.

What else? We had two readings, one by a teacher colleague of Mary's (something vaguely uplifting from Kahlil Gibran) and another by an old boyfriend whose face was faintly familiar (Elizabeth Barrett Browning's 'How do I love thee? Let me count the ways . . .'). We sang, or mouthed, Blake's 'Jerusalem', on the tacit understanding that it had somehow been purged of its religious connotations. Then the curtains parted and the coffin slid away into the industrial processing of death.

At no point did Alan mention me. Nor did he meet my eyes. I had been erased from the story of Mary's life. I was invisible.

There was an order of service, a little booklet with the verses of 'Jerusalem' and the texts of the readings. On the front was a vignetted photograph of Mary, which I looked at while the coffin slid between the curtains to the accompaniment of Robbie Williams's 'Angels'.

The picture must have been taken a year or so earlier. She was smiling at the camera. The light caught the angles of her face – the high cheekbones, the dark eyebrows, the full lower lip; my features as well. Her hair covered most of her forehead, so I couldn't see the scar. Something about the photo suggested that she had been one of a group – a birthday celebration, perhaps, or a reunion. She looked older than she was in my memory. Happier, too.

Everyone, Alan said just before we left, was welcome to join the family for a cup of tea and a sandwich in the village hall, which was two miles away.

We filed out. There was an unspoken etiquette about this – the family went first, for they were at the top of the hierarchy of grief. Then came the close friends, I guessed, then the colleagues from work. Finally, the people in the back rows went outside. People who hadn't known her well. People who were merely curious. People like me, the ghosts from Mary's past.

It was still raining. The wind had risen and the trees between the chapel and the car park were swaying and rustling. The mourners of the next cremation were already arriving and the car park was crowded. Two or three of us paused, waiting to let a car go by.

'I wonder who they've got to do the sandwiches,' said a woman at my elbow, one of the pair who had been sitting in the row in front of me. 'I hope it's Harrell's.'

'Or Thurston's.' Her friend lowered her voice. 'You wouldn't have guessed, would you?'

'That it was . . .?'

'Of course, they couldn't be sure, so they said it was an accident. For the family's sake. You can't blame them, can you?'

They moved away. I hesitated near the exit road. A queue of cars inched towards the main road. A silver Renault paused a few feet away. I glanced at the driver's window and saw Alan looking up at me. The girl was beside him in the front, the boy was in the back.

Alan didn't lower the window. His face was perfectly blank. I raised my hand in a tentative salute. His head turned away. Perhaps I really was invisible. The queue rolled forward.

I went back to my own car, sat behind the wheel and stared at the blurred windscreen. What had I expected? A quiet reconciliation over Mary's body? A tacit agreement that her death must bring us all together?

I became aware that I had something in my hands. I looked down at my lap. I was still holding the order of service. Quite unconsciously, I had rolled it into a cylinder and squeezed it out of shape.

I unrolled the booklet and smoothed it out on my thigh. As it happened, it was face down. There was another photograph on the back, a sort of companion piece to the one on the front.

This one was also a vignette taken from a larger image. It was in black and white and better quality than the one on the front. It showed the Mary I remembered best, her hair scraped back in a ponytail from her forehead. If you'd seen her from the front in those days, you'd have thought she was a boy.

Behind her was part of a wall and the sill of a sash window. I knew with the sharp certainty of childhood memory that she had been standing outside the dining room window, where my father often took photographs of us.

Mary was grinning. There was a lot of detail in the photograph. I could even make out the scar on her fore-head, a squarish indentation, paler than the surrounding skin. She had gashed her head when she fell off the roof of the garden shed.

That hadn't been an accident. Nor, it seemed, had her death.

2

I hadn't seen Mary for thirteen years – not since our mother's final illness and the aftermath of her death. In the ten years before that, she and I had met perhaps half a dozen times, and always in some way because of our parents. Even on that subject, if it was possible for us to disagree, we generally found a way, whether it was the best retirement flat, the best form of medical treatment or even how much milk to put in Mother's tea.

Both of us knew that the real problem lay far deeper than this, in our shared childhood. Mary was more than four years younger than me. She said once that I'd resented her from the moment she was born, purely because she drained our parents' attention away from me. Quite simply, she said, I was jealous.

It's true that four years is a big age gap between children. When we were young, Mary never seemed quite real to me – more like an animated toy I had no desire to play with. A toy that was forever too young for me. Forever unwanted.

There is no doubt that I was unkind to her, on occasions cruel. I did the things that older brothers do to their sisters. I put a spider in her breakfast cereal and a frog in her bed.

I hid one of her school shoes, which made her late for assembly and caused her to get a detention. And I pushed her off the shed roof. That's what caused the little scar on her forehead. She had hit her head on a nail that protruded slightly from the post that supported the washing line.

'I'll get you!' she wailed, blood dripping down her face. 'One day when I'm bigger, I swear it! I hate you!'

It must have been a month or two after that my father took the photograph.

I had learned that Mary was dying about three weeks earlier. Neither she nor Alan told me. It was my aunt, my mother's younger sister, who had married a sergeant in the USAAF and gone to live in Phoenix, Arizona. Mary had emailed her with the news.

My aunt knew of the rift between us, but, even so, she assumed I would have heard about something so momentous. She mentioned it when we were talking on Skype.

'Pancreatic cancer,' she said. 'There are secondaries all over the place – there's nothing they can do. It could be any time, Alan said.'

She began to cry and I saw the tears trickling down her cheek four thousand miles away.

'Sorry,' she said, and blew her nose. 'I'm better now.'

I phoned them. First I talked to Mary's boy, my nephew, Matthew, who appeared not to know who I was. Perhaps he didn't. He fetched his father.

'Yes,' Alan said. 'She is dying. No, she doesn't want to see you and, to be honest, nor do the rest of us. She says you've done enough harm.'

He cut the connection. I went online immediately and googled the hospitals within a twenty-mile radius of her home. I tried them all, but none of them had Mary among their patients.

The next day I widened the search, concentrating on the big hospitals. I found Mary at last in Addenbrooke's in Cambridge. I telephoned the ward and, when I said I was her brother, they put me through to the room, telling me not to talk for long and not to tire her.

But Alan picked up the phone.

'Go away,' he said. 'Can't you leave her in peace?'

What happened after Mother died was not my fault. Her estate consisted of the bungalow in Norwich, about £50,000 in savings and a motley collection of shares inherited from my father and an uncle with a taste for dabbling on the stock exchange.

Alan wanted the bungalow for his own father, who was coming down to live with them. The valuation of the shares and the savings was roughly equivalent to that of the bungalow and its contents, so it seemed obvious that I should have the money and Mary the house.

The last time I saw Mary was when we met to discuss the division of the estate. It wasn't a cordial meeting – we were never comfortable together – but it was perfectly amicable and businesslike.

Four months after the distribution of the estate, a small, almost moribund confectionery company in the Midlands was taken over by a multinational conglomerate that wanted two of its products for their own. I had inherited a block of shares in the confectionery company. The sale made their worth rocket to five or six times their previous value.

Mary and Alan were convinced I had masterminded the whole thing, that I had had advance knowledge of the company sale. I offered them half of the profit, although I had no obligation to do so. They turned it down.

It wasn't rational. Mary preferred to believe a lie and to be out of pocket because of it. But of course, it wasn't about the money at all. It was about the spider in her cereal and the frog in her bed. It was about the shed roof and the nail.

I didn't see Mary again. But I did hear from her. Four days after my abortive attempt to phone her at Addenbrooke's, my mobile bleeped.

I was alone in the house – Beth, my wife, was in New York. When the text arrived, I was chopping broccoli on the kitchen counter and half-listening to a resolutely unfunny comedy programme on the radio.

Knife in hand, I glanced at the phone, which was by the chopping board. The screen had lit up and there was a message from a mobile number I didn't recognize: Go away. I hate you.

3

By the time I left the crematorium, everyone else had gone and the cars for someone else's funeral had refilled the car park.

I had no desire to join them in the village hall, so I set off for home – or rather, towards Ipswich, where I had booked a room in a Travelodge for the night. I had an appointment nearby with a client first thing in the morning, and afterwards I planned to drive back to London.

That was the idea. But the journey went wrong from the start. There were roadworks and I took several wrong turns. My mind was on Mary, not navigation, and I managed to get myself thoroughly lost.

By now it was the provincial equivalent of rush hour. I joined a line of traffic crawling behind a mechanical digger a hundred yards ahead. Darkness fell, the light leaching slowly from the pale grey dome of the East Anglian sky. The rain grew steadily heavier. After nearly an hour we passed a junction with another main road and the digger turned aside. But afterwards the traffic moved almost as slowly as ever.

It was seven o'clock before I found myself on the A12, which runs roughly parallel with the coast down to

Ipswich. I was miles out of my way. How I had got there, I have no idea. I soon discovered that the A12 is not a fast road. You are at the mercy of whatever lies ahead of you.

A sign loomed up by the side of the road: *Put British Pork on Your Fork*.

The headlights of passing vehicles swept over the field beside the sign. The beams revealed hundreds of arcs made of corrugated iron standing in a sea of mud.

It was a pig farm. I had seen several of them on the drive up to Norwich in the morning. It looked like a prison camp, but perhaps, compared to the solitude and confinement of a traditional sty, it was a porcine paradise.

On the other hand, some or possibly all of the pigs had broken out of paradise. The headlights ahead picked out at least half a dozen of them in the middle of the road and others rootling on the grass verges. The stream of cars was slowing. Then it stopped.

For a minute or two I sat there, watching the wipers slapping to and fro across the windscreen. No traffic was coming from the opposite direction. When she was very small, Mary had had a thing about pigs. She had pigs on her wallpaper, pigs on her duvet, pigs on her favourite mug. I used to call her 'Piggy' and make grunting noises, which enraged her – partly, I think now, because she liked pigs so much that she almost wanted to be one.

Two drivers in the queue ahead had left their cars and were discussing the hold-up. I grabbed my umbrella and went to join them.

'It's at least half a mile solid up there,' one of them told me with gloomy pride. 'Them bloody pigs are all over the shop. They made an artic jackknife right across the road. That's why nothing's bloody getting through.'

The other one was looking ahead, peering through the rain. 'They're turning off up there.'

He was right. Ahead of us, cars were peeling away one by one from the main road and turning left.

'Seawick Road,' said the first one. 'You can cut through that way – work your way back to the A12 a mile or two south.'

A car overtook us, followed by a second and a third. They all turned left. Other drivers had had the same idea.

The second man said, 'Could be hours before they clear this lot. Where are the police when you want them?'

'I ain't waiting around for them. I'm late for tea already and it's my eldest's birthday.'

They went back to their cars, and so did I. When they pulled out of the line, I joined them. There's nothing so tedious as waiting in a queue. The first man was a local and clearly knew the way. All I had to do was follow. Besides, I had a satnav program on my phone, so, if the worst came to the worst, I could always find my own way back to the A12.

That was my first mistake. Perhaps the pigs were an omen, if only I'd had the sense to see it.

4

At first everything was easy. I congratulated myself on my cleverness. I followed the tail lights of the car ahead and had the reassurance of other people's headlights behind me. The road was narrow and winding. There was a good deal of surface water, which threw up spray as the cars passed through it.

We came to a large puddle that stretched across the whole road. The cars ahead edged through it. The two I was following were both four-wheel drives, high off the road. I gave them a few seconds and then followed even more slowly in my little Honda.

I reached the other side in safety. But because of the delay the tail lights ahead were no longer visible. Nor were the headlights behind – perhaps the other cars had turned off, rather than risk the puddle.

By now it was completely dark. It was still raining. I drove on for half a mile. The road passed through dense woodland, a conifer plantation perhaps. There were no lights to be seen.

I stopped at the side of the road. I turned on the phone and pressed the icon for the maps program. It began to load, then froze. I waited a moment. Nothing happened.

It was then that I noticed on the top left-hand corner of the screen the words *No Service*.

This was tiresome, but no more than that. If I drove on I would come to a signpost or, at the very least, a house where I could ask the way. Or the black spot would end and my phone would start working again. Unfortunately, I didn't have a road atlas in the car, but I knew I was somewhere between the A12 to the west and the North Sea to the east. The strip of land between them was relatively narrow, so I could hardly get seriously lost. I had nearly half a tank of petrol. True, I was growing hungry – I rather regretted turning up my nose at the sandwiches in the village hall – but once I was back on the A12 I would soon find a pub or café where I could stop for a snack.

I drove off again. My world contracted to the interior of the car and the twin cones of the headlights, diagonally slashed with rain. The road narrowed to a lane. It left the wood and wound between hedges. It acquired a slight but perceptible downward gradient.

The car lurched. And again. And again. And again.

I swore and braked. There was a puncture on the near-side rear tyre. I had probably picked it up when I had stopped at the side of the road to try the phone.

I pulled over, cut the engine and opened the glove compartment. There was a torch in there, though I hadn't used it for months. I flicked the switch and, to my relief, the bulb lit.

I switched on the hazard lights and climbed out of the car. The wind had got up in the last hour or so. It snatched the door from my hands and threw it open. A squall of rain hit my face. I tried to raise the umbrella – it was one of Beth's, a cheap one designed for a handbag – and the wind immediately blew it inside out.

I swore loudly. I dropped the remains of the umbrella

on the floor of the car and made my way to the back. I kept an old waxed jacket in the boot. I shrugged it on – it was clammy and heavy, but it gave some protection against the weather.

It was years since I had changed a tyre, but it was a perfectly straightforward job unless the wheel nuts were screwed on too tightly. I pulled up the base of the boot to take out the spare.

Only then did I remember that the Honda didn't have a spare tyre. To save space and weight, the designers had substituted a little repair kit that was supposed to provide a temporary remedy for a puncture, enough to get you to the nearest garage. I had no idea how this kit worked and I was pretty sure that trying to use it in the rain and darkness would get me nowhere.

That left me with two options: settle down, cold and hungry, and spend the night in the car; or try to find help.

I didn't have much choice. At this point the road was wide enough to leave the car where it was – there was room for traffic to pass, assuming any traffic wanted to. I fastened the jacket up to my chin, locked the Honda and set off down the lane, pursued by the orange pulse of the hazard lights.

After fifty yards or so, the road swung left. The flashing lights vanished. I was alone with the rain and the sound of my own footsteps.

I had forgotten how dark it can be in the country. It's never dark in London. I've always been a city-dweller. There were neither stars nor a moon. The torch beam shone directly in front of me, illuminating the surface of the road. It gave off such an inadequate and partial light that it had the paradoxical effect of emphasizing the darkness rather than dispelling it.

It was also very quiet. That wasn't something I was used to, either. I heard my footsteps and the rustle of the rain and the wind. There was another sound, a faint but continuous roar that came and went in the distance, growing steadily louder.

The sea.

As I turned the corner the wind leapt at me with extra force, nearly knocking me over. It was so violent, so elemental, that I stopped in my tracks and wondered whether to retreat to the car.

It was then that I saw the light, a speck in the darkness. It was difficult to measure the distance, but it looked about a hundred yards away.

I cupped my hands and shouted. The wind blew my words back at me. I set off towards the light, forcing myself to a stumbling run, the torchlight wavering in front of me.

Almost at once the surface of the lane deteriorated. The tarmac gave way to what felt like mud interspersed with the occasional island of hard core. Rain soaked the lower part of my trousers. My face was wet. When I licked my lips I tasted the tang of salt.

The sea was very close now, its rolling roar angrier and louder. That was the moment I realized that this ridiculous adventure was no longer just time-wasting and inconvenient. It was becoming increasingly unpleasant. I was even growing a little scared. This was not a night to be outside, especially not in the middle of nowhere.

The lane ended in a gate with a stile beside it. The source of the light was somewhere beyond it. It seemed no closer than it had been before.

I passed through the stile and into a field that sloped down towards what I assumed was the sea. The surface was too uneven for running in the dark – I didn't want to sprain an ankle – so I slowed to a walk. The force of the wind was stronger here. It wrapped itself around me, pushing me away from the light. The grinding of the sea filled my ears.

I heard a cry. Just for a moment – a high wordless sound, instantly swallowed by the sea. It could have been human. Or from a bird or a fox. It was a cry, that's all, barely audible in all the racket and devoid of personality.

The light was nearer now, a faint yellow glow. I shone the torch ahead. This time, as well as the slivers of rain, it picked out what looked like masonry. The light was to the left of it and beyond it, on the seaward side.

I drew closer. The masonry resolved itself into the flint and rubble you see so much in old East Anglian buildings. But the closer I got, the more I suspected this wasn't the remains of a barn. The torch played over pieces of dressed stone among the rubble and flint. I ran the beam up the side of a pier that rose up beside an arch so high above me that the torchlight gave out before it got there.

It was a fragment of something much grander. A church or a manor house, perhaps. I followed the line of it towards the light. There were three big openings in the wall. Then there was a small, single-storey cottage embedded in the side of the ruin. It had two windows, one on either side of the door.

The nearer window was uncurtained. On the sill was the source of the light I had followed – a hurricane lamp.

I knocked on the door. Nothing happened. I knocked again, more loudly. I stood back to wait and accidentally nudged a covered bucket on the path by the door. The lid fell off with a metallic clatter. I smelled something rotten, something foul.

The lantern suddenly disappeared from the windowsill. A bolt scraped back. The door opened, but only about three inches, and a strip of light made a stripe across the doorstep and touched my sodden shoes.

A woman said, 'Who is it?'

'I'm sorry to bother you,' I said. 'My car's broken down. Could I possibly use your phone?'

'We haven't got one.' Her voice trembled slightly.

It occurred to me that she might be alone in the cottage. It was a foul night and she would naturally be suspicious of a strange man turning up on her doorstep at this hour.

'I'm sorry to bother you,' I said again. 'But I need to find help.'

I couldn't see much of her, because she had angled the lamp so it shone on me. I had the impression of dark hair and thin, pointed features. She didn't look directly at me. She had turned her head so her face was almost in profile.

'Are you all right?' I said.

'Yes, perfectly.' There was a trace of a foreign accent. 'Well, actually – no. I've got an awful cold. Look, if you want a phone, the Mortons have got one. If you go back up to the gate, then follow the line of the hedge, there's a footpath that goes into the bottom of the garden.' She began to close the door. 'There's a gate. You can't miss it.'

'Is it far?' I said.

'No. Ten minutes' walk if you—' she broke off. 'Did you hear that?'

We listened. All I heard was the rain and the wind and the restless movements of the sea.

'What was it?' I said.

'I thought I heard a bell. Sorry, I must go. Goodbye.'

Before I could reply, she closed the door. As I turned away she tilted her head to look at me and the lamplight caught her face. I thought I glimpsed a bruise or perhaps a birthmark on her left cheek.

The bolt rattled home on the other side of the door. I waited a few seconds. She replaced the lantern on the windowsill, but this time she drew the curtain. I half-wished that I had looked through the window before knocking on the door. But there would have been something prurient about spying on her.

I braced myself and plodded up the field, away from

the cottage. It was easier than I had expected, mainly because the weather was now behind me, not in front of me. The wind and the rain made a cushion of pressure that pushed me away from the sea.

I wondered about the woman. Probably young rather than old. Perhaps she was Polish or Czech or something – there had definitely been an intonation in her voice that wasn't English, though in other respects her accent was rather prim and clipped. Lots of farms employed seasonal workers from other parts of Europe. She could be one of those, though it wasn't the time of year you'd expect much casual work on a farm. Or she might be an artist. I hadn't seen any sign of another person. She had said that 'we' hadn't got a phone. But that might have been just to make me think someone else was about the place.

The gate loomed up ahead of me. I paused by the hedge to get my bearings. I couldn't see the cottage and the ruin beside it. The light had gone from the window, which gave me a pang, a sense of loss. There was nothing there at all now – just the darkness, the wind and the rain, and the growling sea.

Then I heard it, too: the sound of the bell, almost swallowed up by the weather. A single note. That was all.

5

The Mortons' house lay in a gentle hollow, sheltered from the weather by a belt of trees. I walked through what looked like a vegetable garden, over a leaf-strewn lawn towards the house. I headed for an outside light fixed to one corner of the building. Once I was round the corner I saw the front of the house. It was a substantial place, Edwardian perhaps or a little later, of a type you could find in the leafier suburbs of any city.

Most windows of the main rooms faced away from the sea towards another lawn, this one bordered by a shrubbery. There were lights behind the curtains in three of the windows. A gravel drive skirted the lawn and widened in front of the house. A Volvo estate was parked outside. Beyond the house was what looked like a garage block detached from the main building.

I went into the tiled porch and rang the bell. The door was half-glazed, with a stained-glass panel. The light was on in the hall. I stood there, shivering. It was only then, now I was out of the rain and the wind for the first time in what seemed hours, that I realized how cold and wet I was. I passed my fingers through my hair in a crude attempt to comb it. A puddle formed around my feet.

A blurred shape approached the door. I heard the rattle of a chain – they were a suspicious lot in this part of Suffolk. The door opened a couple of inches.

'Yes?' A woman's voice, hard and suspicious.

I explained what had happened.

'The lady over there' – I nodded towards the sea – 'said you might allow me to use your phone. Your landline.'

'There's a fault on the line, I'm afraid. It's the weather.'

I took out my mobile. I still had no signal.

'Do you have a mobile I could borrow for a moment? I'd happily pay for—'

'You won't get a mobile to work here,' she said in the same flat voice. 'Any mobile. No coverage.'

'Who is it, Jane?'

A shape moved behind the stained glass. It was another woman, but, judging by her voice, older than the first.

'He says his car has broken down,' Jane said, turning away. 'He wanted to use the phone, but it's not working.'

'Where is your car?' the old woman said – speaking to me, though I still couldn't see her, except as a shifting blur of colour in the stained glass.

'It sounds absurd, but I'm not quite sure.'

I tried the effect of a rueful smile on Jane, but her face didn't soften. I explained about the ill-fated diversion from the A12 and the migrating pigs, about getting lost and about the puncture.

'I left the car in the lane and walked down to the field by the sea at the end. I—'

'It sounds to me as if you've left your car on Picton Lane,' the old woman said. 'Open the door, Jane.'

'Are you sure?' Jane looked back into the hall. 'He's . . . terribly wet.'

111

She wasn't worried about the water. She was worried about letting a strange man into their house.

'Quite sure, dear.'

Jane took the door off the chain and held it open. I stepped into the warmth and light of the hall. She was a sturdy woman, perhaps twenty years older than me. She was as tall as I was and considerably heavier. She glared at me. I smiled back.

'Stand on the mat. Not on the carpet,' she said. 'Please.'

'Fetch a towel, dear,' the other woman said.

Jane looked at me, but she did what she was told. The older woman was thin, her body bent over with something like osteoporosis. She looked as if you could knock her over with the flick of a finger or just by blowing hard at her. She was leaning on a white stick.

'Would you come over here?' she said, tapping the stick on the floor.

'But the carpet? I'm very wet.'

'Never mind the carpet.' Her voice was vigorous even if her body wasn't. 'Come here.'

I took three steps forward, which brought me immediately in front of her.

'Do you mind if I feel your face? I'm blind.'

'Of course not.'

She lifted her right hand and found first my shoulder, then my neck and finally my face. Her fingertips fluttered over it, as gentle as the touch of a cobweb.

'Yes,' she said, and dropped her hand. 'Yes. Thank you.'

There were footsteps. The door opened and Jane reappeared with a towel.

'Oh, Mother,' she said. 'He's dripped everywhere.'

'It doesn't matter.'

'Look, I'm sorry,' I said. 'I'm in the way. I'll go back to my car – unless there's somewhere else which might have a working phone?'

'You can't spend the night in your car. Jane would take you into Southwold, but our car's out of action.' She smiled at me. 'Like that wretched phone. You'll have to spend the night here.'

'Mother!'

'I couldn't possibly—'

'Nonsense.' She shut us both up. 'If you go blundering about in this weather and then try and sleep in wet clothes in your car you'll end up catching pneumonia. I'm not having that on my conscience.' She gave a dry chuckle. 'I've quite enough on my conscience as it is.'

Jane said, 'The bed in the garage is made up. I suppose he could sleep there.'

'Good idea.' The older woman smiled at me. 'It's not quite as primitive as it sounds. We had the loft converted into a holiday apartment.'

'Thank you.' I gave her a smile she couldn't see. 'I'd happily sleep in a haystack as long as it was out of the rain and the wind.'

'If you're spending the night with us, we'd better get to know each other.' She held out her hand. 'I'm Christina Morton. This is my daughter, Jane.'

I told her my name and all three of us shook hands in the strangely formal way that Mrs Morton felt appropriate for these unusual circumstances.

Now the decision to shelter me had been taken, Jane made the best of it. She took me through to the kitchen, which was blessedly warm with an Aga. She made me a cup of tea and hung up my waxed jacket. She raised her eyebrows when she saw the dark suit I was wearing.

'Not ideal for country rambles,' she said.

'I was on my way back from a funeral,' I said.

'You'd better give me the suit to hang up. I'll find you something of my husband's to wear while it's drying.'

113

While I finished my tea, she went away for a moment. She came back with an old pair of jeans and a jersey, together with a pair of socks. She held up the jeans in front of me, narrowing her eyes like a shop assistant.

'They'll do. David was larger than you, but I daresay you won't mind that.'

She made a hot-water bottle to air the bed and took me to the apartment. On our way out, we passed through a lobby beside the kitchen, with rows of clothes and boots. She picked out a pair of wellingtons and an elderly raincoat that she said had belonged to her father.

A side door led from the lobby to the back of the garage block on the other side of a yard. A flight of outside steps led up to the apartment above. It was small, with sloping ceilings. Most of the space was taken up by a sitting room lit by a pair of dormer windows. Beyond it was a bedroom, just large enough for a double bed, with an en suite shower room and a lavatory. The air was cold and a little damp.

Jane left me there – 'to settle in' – telling me to come back to the kitchen in half an hour for supper.

'Just a sandwich or something. We don't have much in the evening – Mother goes to bed early.'

When she had gone I prowled about the apartment, as one does in a strange place, opening cupboards and drawers. There was a shelf of books – mainly the sort that people buy for holiday reading and then discard – and an elderly TV with a DVD player below. In one drawer I found a heap of children's drawings, crude crayon sketches. One of them showed a pair of ruined archways with two stick-like figures in front of it. I wondered if it was a child's view of the ruins in the field beyond the garden.

I was putting on the boots again to go over to the house when there was a knock on the door. Jane was outside, holding a tray.

114

'I'm sorry,' she said. 'Mother's not feeling well and I'm going to put her to bed.'

She held out the tray to me and automatically I took it.

'Do you mind having your supper here? It'll make life easier.'

'Of course not. Is there anything I can do to help?'

'No, nothing. It's just old age, I think. There's a jug of fresh milk there – you found the kettle? Tea and coffee in the cupboard over the sink. Breakfast at eight.'

I thanked her and she went away. I set down the tray. There were cheese sandwiches, a slice of fruitcake and an apple. There was even a bottle of beer. I realized how ravenous I was. I had had nothing since a bowl of soup in a pub at lunchtime.

I sat down at the table and wolfed the food. Afterwards, I sat with the beer and flicked through the TV channels. There was nothing I wanted to watch. Mary's funeral had stirred up memories that were better left in peace. I didn't allow myself to dwell on them – what would be the point? What's done is done and you can never go back, can you? But they formed a sort of uncomfortable static in the background of my mind that prevented me from settling to anything else. I had never liked Mary much and it seemed somehow typical that even in death she should have found a way to torment me.

Gradually there stole over me a sense of disconnectedness. It's hard to explain. We live such ordered lives, so carefully filled with the things we must do and the things we think we want to do, that we lose the knack of coping with the absence of organization. Mary's funeral and its tiresome and time-wasting sequel this evening had combined to take away the comfortable structure in which I usually live. It was as if I had been removed from my own life and transplanted into someone else's, someone I didn't know.

The fact that my phone wouldn't work seemed to sum it up. I couldn't use it to read the paper or browse the Internet. I couldn't call anyone or email them or text them. I wondered how people had managed in the past, with all this emptiness, all this silence, all this time on their hands. I was alone with myself and I wasn't sure I liked it.

I got up. I turned out the light and went to the nearer of the two dormer windows. This one looked out on to the back of the house. I opened the curtain and put my face against the dark glass.

At first I saw nothing. Then I made out the dense shadow of the house and the pale grey of the sky above. There were no lights visible. Either the Mortons were at the front of the house or they were already asleep.

I crossed the room to the other window. This one faced the seaward side, though one wouldn't have known it, even in the daylight, because it was concealed by the trees at the bottom of the garden and by the fold of land beyond.

It occurred to me that my sister would have liked this place. When we were children she had always wanted us to move to the country. Unlike most children, she'd liked the darkness. I never found out why. It didn't occur to me to be curious until it was too late.

I didn't want to think about Mary. That's why I opened the window – as a distraction. I stuck my hand outside. The air was cool, but not as cold as I had expected. It seemed to have stopped raining.

I rested my elbows on the sill and stared into the darkness. The night was full of noises. The trees rustled. My eyes slowly adjusted and I saw the tops of the trees swaying in the wind. Beyond that was another, more menacing noise: the roar of the sea, pulsing in its strange inhuman rhythm against the land.

The sound had a hypnotic effect – I was growing chilly in front of the open window, but I didn't move. I stayed there until I heard another sound, so distant and so faint that the other noises of the night almost drowned it: the irregular tolling of a bell.

6

Ten minutes later, I went outside.

Boredom had something to do with it, as did the sense that for a few short hours I had taken an enforced holiday from my ordinary life. I wanted to do something different, to be someone different. I wanted to pretend I was a different sort of person, more adventurous and more curious than I really was. Above all, I wanted to stop thinking about Mary.

So I put on the raincoat and boots of the absent and presumably dead Mr Morton, picked up my torch and another one which went with the apartment, and opened the door. For a moment I hesitated, held back by an innate sense of caution. I couldn't hear the bell any more. Perhaps it was mounted on a buoy miles offshore and the movements of the sea accounted for the irregularity of the tolling.

I went outside and closed the door. The wind tugged at the long skirts of Mr Morton's raincoat. I listened to the weather and felt it on the skin of my face.

I followed the torch beam down the steps, moving as quietly as I could to lessen the risk of disturbing the two women. For the same reason, when I reached the bottom of the steps, I avoided the house. Rather than go towards the lawn at the front, in which case the gravel would amplify my footsteps, I went through an archway in the wall just beyond the garages. There was a sort of orchard here, through which a path led to the vegetable garden and then to the trees at the end of the garden.

I was using the Mortons' torch, which was larger and had a much more powerful beam than mine. I stood beside the fence beyond the trees and sent its light swooping over the field. It was much noisier here. Though the rain had slackened off, the wind was whipping up the sea to a frenzy.

The beam's reach stopped far short of the cottage by the ruins. It was only then that I decided to walk in that direction. Up to this point I had had no goal beyond the idea of going outside. Now it seemed logical that I should give myself a goal: I would walk over to the cottage and back. That would give a shape to my little adventure in the dark, and the exercise would help me sleep better.

I went through the gate and walked slowly along the line of the fence until I reached the opening to the lane. From here I could see the cottage or, rather, a faint light that must come from there.

I set off towards it. I made slower progress now because I was walking into the wind. The grass – some sort of pasture, I assumed – was rough and uneven, slippery with the rain. Mr Morton's wellingtons were too big for me and my feet slithered in their cold interior.

I admit: there was another reason for me to go towards the cottage. I was curious about the woman I had seen there. There was nothing sexual in my interest. I didn't want to play the peeping Tom. I just wanted to know why she – and perhaps someone else? – had chosen to live in such an isolated place. I wanted to know where she came from and what she did. I wanted to see her properly. I wanted to find out if that mark on her face was a birthmark or a bruise.

It's odd how the mind works. The mark had lodged in my memory without my being aware of it. Remembering it now, I found it reminded me of something else, something vaguely unsettling though quite different, that was just beyond my grasp.

All this time I was moving slowly towards the sea, my head bent into the wind. A more forceful gust than usual made me stagger and almost fall. As I steadied myself, I discovered that the distraction had unclogged the blockage in my memory.

The woman's blemish reminded me of another: the scar on my sister's forehead. Rationally, of course, there was no connection between them whatsoever. But some part of my mind insisted that somehow there was.

The three arches of the ruin loomed up. The torch beam played over them. Part of the church, I decided, definitely not a house. I approached the cottage as quietly as I could. I didn't imagine that the woman had many nocturnal visitors and I didn't want to scare her.

The front of the cottage came into sight. The light was coming not from the window, as before, but from the doorway. The door itself was open and the glow of a lamp splashed on to the brick path outside.

That was odd – after all, no one would want to leave an outside door open in this weather. Perhaps she had gone out to fetch more logs – from my glimpse earlier in the evening, the house had struck me as the sort of place that would have a wood-burning stove as standard equipment – and the door had blown open.

At that point I almost walked away – back to the Mortons' house, back to the apartment over the garage with its television and its electric kettle and its shelf of holiday paperbacks. It was none of my business what the woman was up to and I was pretty sure she wouldn't want me intruding in whatever it was.

But I didn't walk away. When Mary had fallen off the shed I had walked away, leaving her crying her heart out with pain and shock on the path. There had been spots of blood on the concrete. Colour-coded accusations. She and I had both known that I was as guilty as hell, and that soon our parents would know it too. (I realized, years later, that this was precisely what Mary had wanted from the start.)

I walked softly along the front of the cottage. I called out, in the absurd way we do, 'Excuse me?' when what I really meant to say was, 'Hello? Anyone there? Are you OK? I don't want to frighten you.'

No one answered. The words lingered, foolish and empty in my ears. I walked forward until the light from the door spilled on to my glistening wellingtons, then my legs and then enveloped me entirely.

'Hello?' I called, much more quietly now because I had seen what lay within.

The door opened directly into a living room. Although it was lit only by a single hurricane lamp, it was obvious it was in a mess. The storm seemed to have passed through it rather than above and over it.

In the far corner was a table scattered with papers and books, some of which had ended up on the floor. There were a couple of old kitchen chairs, one of which had been knocked over. The dominant feature of the room was an enormous sofa, which looked as if it had been thrown out of someone's drawing room about half a century ago and spent the intervening years sliding down the social scale. It was almost six feet long and had a sagging seat enclosed by a high back and sides. The arms were faced with panels of mahogany that gleamed, dull and red, in the lamplight. There was a blanket on it and another blanket on the floor.

The sofa stood almost on top of a blackened stove set in a large inglenook fireplace that filled most of the wall to the right of the doorway. I took a step towards it and stumbled on a book lying on the floor. Automatically I stooped and picked it up. It was an old hardback written in German, a language I don't know. But I read the title, *Zeit und Wahrheit*, and I knew what *Zeit* meant, at least: time.

I put the book on the table and looked around. I was uneasy, of course – quite apart from the abandoned state of the place, I had the unpleasant sensation you get when you enter someone else's empty home: as if you are an interloper, an invader of privacy; it's even worse when you enter uninvited and as a complete stranger.

The hurricane lamp didn't throw out much light. I panned the torch around the room, which was low-ceilinged and little more than twelve feet square. The beam picked out more details in its harsh light. The brick floor. An ashtray overflowing with cigarette ends. A glass on the windowsill. And a long curtain – no, a blanket – that stretched from floor to ceiling in the middle of the wall opposite the stove.

I lifted the side of the blanket. It was acting as a draught excluder over a door. I knocked on it, waited a moment, then called out: 'Hello? Is anyone there?'

A rustling made me spin round. The draught from outside had caught one of the sheets of paper on the floor and sent it skittering across the room.

I raised the latch on the door, pushed it open and let the light of the torch go before me.

'Anyone there?'

Immediately on the right was an alcove which was obviously used as a sort of kitchen. There was a stone sink, with shelves and cupboards above, and a primus stove. On the left was another, smaller alcove with a pile

122

of firewood below a row of hooks for coats. In front of me was a wall with another blanket hanging on it.

'Hello?'

I pulled the blanket aside. There was no door behind it, only a room a little smaller than the one with the sofa. The air was even colder here and smelled strongly of mould. Much of the space was taken up with an unmade double bed with a dark wooden headboard. There was another inglenook fireplace, this one with a grate designed for logs and a pile of ash spreading out on to the hearth. The torch picked out a bookcase, a vase on the window-sill containing two very dead roses that had lost most of their petals, another ashtray by the bed on top of a pile of books, an old chair strewn with clothes and—

A white face appeared, above a dazzling light. I almost dropped the torch. I realized soon enough what it was: my reflection in a mirror hanging on the wall. But the knowledge didn't stop my heart racing.

I went back to the living room. Whoever lived here had left in a hurry. No one leaves their front door open at night, even in darkest Suffolk, and especially not on a night like this. The place was in chaos. It was beyond squalor.

Who were these people? Hippies going back to nature? Artists with souls far above their creature comforts? Squatters? Illegal immigrants?

I remembered the woman I had met in the evening, how her voice had shaken, how she had heard a bell, how she had wanted to get rid of me. I had known even then that something was wrong, but I had been too trapped in my own predicament to take much notice.

I crossed the living room to the front door. The sound of the wind and the sea was much louder here.

What was I going to do? I couldn't call the police. It was no use my waking the Mortons, as their car was out of service. I could walk back to my own car and drive on

123

a flat tyre until I found myself somewhere that had a phone signal or some sign of human life. But I would have to go back to the Mortons' apartment first, because I had left my useless phone in the pocket of my suit jacket, together with the car keys and my wallet.

Underneath it all was the thought that I might well be raising the alarm for nothing – that there might be a perfectly innocent explanation for this, if only I knew what it was. I had found nothing sinister. All I had found was an empty cottage, admittedly in a mess and with an open door, but those aren't evidence of a crime in themselves. There was no sign that someone had been injured. No sign of theft.

I heard footsteps.

I swung round. The sudden movement made me dizzy. I clung to the jamb of the door for support. For an instant, everything went dark, as if my sight had been snatched away from me.

The dizziness passed and my sight returned. In fact, there wasn't much to see beyond the oblong of light from the doorway. But I could hear all right – the sea and the wind and – only just audible above the racket that nature was making – the dragging footsteps.

They were coming not from the ruins but from further down the path along the front of the cottage towards the place where the invisible sea was grumbling and roaring.

'Who's there?'

It was the voice of the woman I had met earlier. Very clipped and with an intonation that wasn't quite English.

'For God's sake – who's there?'

'It's me,' I said. My torch had picked out a pair of wellingtons and the skirts of a long oilskin coat. I didn't want to shine it on her face for fear of dazzling her eyes. Instead, I stepped on to the path and shone the beam on my own face. 'I came earlier, do you remember? You sent me up to the Mortons.'

'But what are you doing here now?'

I lowered the torch. She had stopped a few yards away. She had a torch, too, and its beam slid towards me and caught me in its light. There was a grating sound as she put down the metal bucket on the brick path. The lid was back on, but there was still a trace of that foul smell in the air.

'The Mortons' phone wasn't working,' I said. 'They offered me a bed for the night.'

'But why are you here?'

'It's quite early still.' I was beginning to get a little annoyed with this interrogation. 'I've had a hell of a day, so I thought I'd take a walk to clear the cobwebs away. Then I saw your light and the door was open and the mess inside. I was wondering if I should call the police or—'

'No!' Her voice had risen almost to a shout. She said, more quietly, 'There's no need.'

'Are you OK?'

'I'm perfectly all right, thank you. Except the damn pig escaped. I've been looking for it.'

I goggled at her. 'The pig?'

'The pig. We've got a pig in the sty at the back. Well, it's not ours, actually, it's the Mortons'. The wind blew part of the fence down. I went to feed her and she wasn't there. I hope she hasn't fallen over the cliff somewhere.'

That explained the bucket. Scraps for the pig.

I said, 'Where's your friend? Still looking?'

'It's none of your business,' she said.

The words said one thing, but her voice said another: it dropped almost to a whisper and acquired a sort of wobble to it, like Mary's used to do when she was a kid and about to burst into tears, usually because of something I had done.

I didn't want to think about Mary.

'Look,' I said. 'Why don't you go inside and get warm

125

and dry? If there's anything I can do to help, just tell me. Help you look – whatever. Otherwise I'll go away. It's up to you.'

I stood aside from the door. She came closer. The light from the doorway showed me the whole of her, for the first time.

Now I saw that she was smaller than me, little taller than my shoulder. She wasn't wearing a hat. The rain or perhaps the salt spray had soaked her hair, making it black and glossy, plastering it against her scalp. She glanced up at me as she passed into the cottage. Her features were delicate and regular. I saw the smudge – bruise or birth-mark? – on her cheekbone. But what I really noticed were her eyes, which were large and dark.

She paused in the doorway. For a long moment we looked at each other.

'You'd better come in, I suppose,' she said.

7

The strange thing about what happened next was that so much of it didn't feel strange. It seemed not exactly normal – never that – but natural, in the way that water flowing downhill is natural or the pleasure of eating when you are hungry.

I followed her into the cottage and closed the door. She took off her oilskin and hung it on a peg on the back of the door, leaving it to drip on the floor. Underneath she wore a shabby khaki trench coat, which looked as if it had come from a charity shop, over a grubby white dress.

Not a dress, I realized, as she crouched by the stove a moment later. A nightdress.

She opened the stove door and threw a handful of driftwood inside, followed by a shovelful of coals. There was a kettle on the top of the stove. She lifted it, testing by the weight how much water was in it.

'It's quite hot,' she said. 'It shouldn't take long to boil once the fire gets going. Tea?'

'Yes, please,' I said.

'I'm afraid there's no milk.' She frowned. 'Or sugar.'

'It doesn't matter.'

'We could have cocoa. But it's horrible without milk.'

'And it's even worse without sugar,' I said.

We smiled at each other.

'Tea, then.' She glanced at me. 'Do take your coat off and sit down. Unless you're too cold.'

I took off the coat and hat and hung them on the empty peg next to hers. She went into the kitchen and came back with a teapot and two cups and saucers on a tray. The china was pretty – Art Deco and very delicate; unexpected in this wreck of a place.

She set down the tray on the table and for the first time seemed to notice the untidiness of the room. While I sat watching from the sofa, she picked up the chair that had fallen over and scooped up handfuls of books and papers from the floor.

'Can I help?'

'No.' She looked up. 'I'm Sophia, by the way.'

I told her my name. 'What happened?'

She didn't answer. She gathered up the rest of the papers and dumped them on the table. She picked up the two blankets. She handed one of them to me.

'Put it over you,' she said. 'It's so horribly cold. It never gets warm here. Or hardly ever.'

She sat down beside me and wrapped her own blanket around her. She was shivering. We listened to the weather and sea and the fuel settling in the stove and the sound of each other's breathing. We both stared at the stove, at the kettle, as if willing it to come to the boil. It was very dim – a single hurricane lamp doesn't throw out much light. To an outsider we must have looked like an old country couple, side by side under our blankets, still in our wellington boots, staring wordlessly at the stove: a tableau of the depressed rural poor, exhausted after the day's drudgery.

'We had a quarrel, you see,' she said.

There was no warning. She didn't look at me. She might have been talking to herself.

128

'Who did?'

'Max and I.' Sophia shifted on the sofa. 'It's not unusual.'

'Is he your husband?'

'My lover.'

A native English-speaker would have said 'my partner', I thought. 'Where is he, then?'

'He walked out.'

'In this weather?'

'That was probably part of the reason.' She touched the cheekbone where the bruise was. 'He likes the grand gesture.'

'You must be worried. Do you want me to go and look, or—'

'No, no, no. I've already been down to the beach. I had to, when I was looking for the pig. So I looked for Max, too. He can't be at the Mortons', or you would have heard him or seen him.' Her lips twitched. 'Probably both, knowing Max. So that means he's gone down the coast path again. You know the cottages at Seawick End? There's a woman in one of them, a widow. I think he goes to her. The bastard.' She turned her head. 'What about you?'

'What do you mean?'

'Are you married?'

'Yes. My wife's in New York.'

I paused. Sophia stared at me in silence.

I said, 'I haven't seen her for six weeks.' I didn't add that her secondment to the firm's New York office was by way of a trial separation for us; and, if the trial worked, that the separation might become permanent.

'Do you miss her?' Sophia said.

I answered as honestly as I could. 'No. Yes. I don't know.'

'What's her name?'

'Beth.'

Sophia got up and, still draped in a blanket, looked at the kettle, which was obstinately refusing to boil.

She turned and looked down at me. 'It always takes ages when you watch it.' She wrapped her arms around her body. She was still trembling.

'Come and sit down,' I said. 'Shall I put more wood on the stove?'

'It won't help. Not until it's hotter.'

She went into the kitchen and came back with a bottle. There was a soft plop as she pulled out the cork.

'I'm going to have some whisky. Do you want some?'

'All right.'

I watched her moving across to the table. She poured whisky into the teacups, left the bottle on the table and brought the cups to the sofa. The light from the lamp was so dim that I could barely make out her features until she sat down beside me.

'There's no soda. Do you want water?'

'No, thanks.' I would have liked ice, but I didn't think there was much point in asking for it.

She raised her cup. 'Cheers,' she said in a precise little voice.

The first mouthful of the spirit stung my throat. The second brought warmth. The third, pleasure. Sophia said nothing. She just drank as if it were an unpleasant duty, like swallowing medicine. Then she got up again, fetched the bottle, refilled our cups and put the bottle on the floor beside the arm of the sofa.

'Have you lived here long?' I asked, just to break the silence.

'Since April. Mr Morton lets us have it rent-free in return for some gardening. Oh, and looking after the pig. Not that I've done that very well this evening.'

'But you're not from here?' I said.

'No.' She sipped her whisky but didn't elaborate. 'Max

needs to be somewhere quiet for a while, and we haven't got much money. He's writing a book.'

'Oh? What sort of a book?'

Sophia shrugged. 'Something about time. He's a philosopher, you see. Whenever he tries to explain it to me, he gets cross. It's because I'm stupid.'

'You're not stupid.'

She gave a little snort of laughter. 'You can't say that. You don't know me.'

'I know enough to be sure you're not stupid. Can I ask you something?'

'If you want.'

'I don't mean to be rude. But – that mark on your cheek. What is it?'

Her hand flew up to the place, shielding it from my eyes. 'It's a bruise.'

Neither of us spoke. I watched her.

'Max hit me,' she went on.

'I'm sorry.'

'Why? What can you do about it?'

'I don't know. But I'm sorry he hit you.'

Sophia drew her feet up and turned to sit facing me. One arm was around her knees. She held her teacup in the other hand. As she drank, her dark eyes studied me over the brim. They gleamed, for at this angle the light from the lamp was reflected in them.

'He does it sometimes,' she said, her voice detached, even bored; she might have been talking about someone who had nothing to do with her. 'He gets angry.'

'What about you? What do you do?'

'You ask a lot of questions, don't you?' She smiled to take the sting from the words. 'Just living here takes up most of my time.'

'No electricity?'

'No. I don't mind that, but it's a bore to have to fetch

our water from the Mortons'. They let us have baths, too, which is awfully kind. We have a very nice earth closet, though, round the back near the place where the pig lives. The only thing is, I worry about winter.'

'You can't stay here when it gets really cold. You'll freeze.'

'Why not? I've known worse. Much worse.' She stretched her hand down towards the bottle. 'Let's have some more.'

'I'd better not. I should leave you in peace.'

'Don't go,' she said. 'Not yet.'

She leaned forward with the bottle and poured another inch of whisky into my cup. The trench coat fell open and I saw her long, pale neck rising from her nightdress, as elegant as a swan's. The hand that held the bottle had chapped skin. Her nails were cut short and they looked grubby, like a boy's, though the light was too uncertain for me to be sure. As she came a few inches nearer to me, she brought her smell with her: something dark and almost feral.

'Drink,' she said.

Sophia was holding the bottle in her left hand. As she drew back, the sleeve of that arm slid down. I glimpsed the blur of a faded tattoo on her outer forearm.

She didn't refill her own cup. She put both it and the bottle on the floor. Then she said my name, twice, and stretched out her hands to me.

Afterwards, I stumbled back to the Mortons'. The shingle was slipping and sliding on the beach. The battery of my torch died. The light from the Mortons' torch was growing feeble so I switched it off.

I looked back three times. I saw the light in Sophia's window the first time, but not the second or third. She had bolted the door when I left.

The trees at the end of the Mortons' garden were

132

swaying and rocking. It was raining hard again and my cheeks were wet. I thought about Max, warm and dry in the arms of the widow at Seawick End. I thought what a fool he was.

When I'd left the cottage, I'd hugged Sophia. She kissed me. I said I'd come back in the morning.

'No,' she said and stroked my cheek.

'Later, then. The afternoon.'

'You don't understand.' She stood back, her hand on the door, ready to close it. 'I don't want to see you again. Ever.'

8

I was up by seven, still with the smell of her on my skin. At eight, still unwashed, I went across the yard to the kitchen. Jane was there, laying the breakfast tray on the table. She asked me in a perfunctory way how I had slept. She said she usually had toast and muesli for breakfast and would that do for me?

She wasn't hostile exactly: she merely gave me the impression that I represented a responsibility that she, a busy woman, could have done without and should not have been required to undertake in the first place.

'Mother won't be down this morning,' she said. 'Had a bad night. Coffee or tea?'

She left me at the table with my breakfast, while she took her mother's tray upstairs, along with a neatly folded copy of the *Daily Telegraph*. She was gone nearly fifteen minutes. I had finished eating by the time she returned. There was a spot of colour on each of her cheeks.

'I must be on my way,' I said. 'Leave you in peace.'

'Yes.' She poured herself a cup of coffee. 'Your clothes and shoes are in the scullery. They're pretty much dry by now.'

I stood up. 'I'll go and change.'

When I came back, wearing my own rather rumpled

suit, I made a joke about at least not having had too much to pack. She received this with a stony face.

I took out my wallet. 'You must let me know what I owe you.'

'Mother says there's no charge.'

'But I must pay you. After all, it's a holiday let. Besides, I really don't know what I—'

'No charge,' she repeated. For the first time she looked directly at me. 'It's her house. It's up to her.'

I asked her to pass on my thanks to Mrs Morton and said goodbye. Jane had already left the kitchen by the time I closed the back door.

The storm had blown itself out, though there was a bank of clouds to the east that suggested another might be on the way. The rain had stopped. There were even shafts of sunlight in the distance, shining down like heavenly spotlights.

I had the odd sensation as I walked down the Mortons' garden that, since yesterday evening, I had been on holiday from my everyday life. Part of me didn't want to go home.

Sophia had told me not to come back. She had said that she didn't want to see me again. But I couldn't accept that. I had known from the moment I woke up that I would go to the cottage on my way back to the car. If Max were there, I would say I had lost my way. Or that I was curious about the ruins. But perhaps he would still be at Seawick End. And perhaps Sophia would change her mind about not seeing me again.

I passed from the shelter of the Mortons' trees into the field beyond. A stiff breeze was blowing off the sea. My trousers flapped around my legs. The suit material was thin. I felt the cold air on my skin. The ground was very wet and my black city shoes were soon unpleasantly damp.

I glimpsed the jagged masonry along the top of the ruins. My heart behaved like a teenager's and began to beat faster. But something wasn't right. Twenty yards later, I stopped and stared.

There weren't three arches any more. There were only two. The cottage at the end had completely disappeared.

For an instant I wondered if it could have been washed away during the night. But that was impossible. Anyway, since I'd last been there, what was left of the ruin had been fenced off from the field.

I went up to the fence. It was made of chain mesh, with strands of rusting barbed wire along the top. Weeds, now dying, had grown tall on both sides of it. A faded sign told me to keep out and warned of danger.

The only possible explanation was that I had hallucinated the whole experience: that both my visits to the cottage yesterday had never happened. Which meant, quite simply, that I was going mad.

A little voice in my mind said: 'Perhaps this is Mary's revenge.'

The cliffs on this part of the coast are friable, with a tendency to crumble into the North Sea. I walked to the end of the field and found a sort of natural ramp that led to the beach below. It was covered with banks of fine shingle, moulded by the waves into glistening ridges. I walked along it, slipping and sliding in my almost useless shoes, looking for traces of the cottage. I found nothing but strands of seaweed, fragments of wood, pieces of plastic – the debris washed up by the storm.

The sea was choppy. The water was the colour of café au lait. The wind dug into it and sent flashes of spray that looked like white lace.

Beyond the beach the coastline curved away in a shimmering arc towards a vast slab of a building. A nuclear power station. One of the celestial spotlights sparkled on its white dome.

* * *

The car was where I had left it, parked on a verge up the lane. The battery was flat – I had completely forgotten that I had left the hazard lights on.

Not that it mattered. In the daylight a cluster of roofs was clearly visible less than half a mile away across the heathland covered with blackening heather and stunted, windswept gorse. The roofs belonged to a small farm. The owner let me use her own mobile, which had a signal, to call the breakdown service.

After that I had nothing to do but wait. The mechanic came within half an hour and did a temporary repair on the tyre and put a booster charge into the battery. I followed his van through the lanes to the A12. By lunchtime I'd had the puncture mended and I was driving south.

I didn't go to see my client near Ipswich in the end – I phoned and made some excuse. Instead I went home. It's not like me to turn away work. I have the usual desperation of the self-employed that makes me take almost any job that is offered for fear that, if I turn one down, I shall never be offered another.

But Sophia had changed that, at least for the time being. What had happened last night affected me on a physical level as much as an emotional or intellectual one. It was as if every particle of my body had been poured into a cup and stirred vigorously with a teaspoon. I don't mean what we did on that huge, disintegrating sofa, though that was certainly stirring in another way, even in memory.

The real problem – or rather the heart of disturbance – was this: I had spent about an hour inside a cottage yesterday evening which I now knew simply wasn't there. The cottage didn't exist. Therefore, nor did Sophia.

So where did that leave me? Here or nowhere?

9

I heard the phone ringing inside as I was standing outside looking for my front-door key. Beth and I owned about a third of a small terraced house in Islington. The street was full of more or less identical houses. Many of the inhabitants had fairly interesting jobs in the media. They earned enough to shop at Waitrose and go skiing once or twice a year, but not enough to move to a house that wasn't quite so cramped.

The phone was still ringing when I got inside. I kicked the door shut, dropped the overnight bag I hadn't used and ran down the hall to the kitchen. The phone stopped ringing just as I stretched out my hand to it.

The caller didn't leave a message. But I tried 1471 and I recognized the number. It was Mary and Alan's.

I called back at once. I knew that, if I didn't, then I probably never would.

Alan answered on the second ring. When I told him who I was, he didn't say anything for a moment. I thought he was going to hang up. Then he said my name, but with the sort of upward lift at the end that suggests a question or a sense of surprise dangling at the end of it.

'How are you?' I said, because I couldn't think of anything else to say.

'All right.'

'And the children?'

'Well – hard to say. I don't think it's really sunk in yet. For any of us.'

We ran out of words for a while. This was the nearest to a normal conversation we had had for thirteen years and we were both out of practice.

'She changed her mind,' he said suddenly.

'About what?'

'About you. About seeing you. I should have told you that yesterday.'

'You had other things on your mind,' I said.

'Mary was drifting in and out at the end. When she was awake, she didn't always recognize me. She was in a dream – that was the morphine, the nurse said. Once – it was the day before she died – she woke up and saw me by the bed. And she thought I was you.'

We listened to each other's breathing for a moment. Five minutes earlier, my head had been full to bursting with Sophia and what had happened yesterday evening. Now Mary had elbowed her way in and I didn't want her there.

'She was pleased to see you,' Alan went on. 'No, not exactly pleased. Anyway, strictly speaking, she didn't see you, of course, she saw me. She – she was excited. She said your name several times and then she said, "It's never too late. There's always a next time."' Alan made a sound that resembled a snort. 'The next time she surfaced, I was back to being me – I must say, I was rather relieved. They let her come home at the end. Did I tell you?'

'No,' I said, thinking of what I had overheard the women say in the car park at the crematorium. 'How was she? At – at the end, I mean?'

He said nothing for a while. When he next spoke it was as if he hadn't heard the question. 'And what about you? How's Beth?'

'She's in New York for a month or two. Work.'

'Good. Good.' Another pause. 'I suppose I'd better go.'

'Alan?'

'What?'

'You're pretty strong on local history, aren't you?'

'Well yes.' He sounded surprised and I didn't blame him. 'I suppose so.'

'And wasn't your PhD something to do with the Middle Ages?'

'Yes.' Now he sounded suspicious. 'The wool trade from 1350 to 1430, since you ask. But I really—'

'I got lost on my way home and I came across some ruins. Somewhere near Southwold, I think. A few miles away. Just a couple of arches on a clifftop in the middle of nowhere.'

'Dunwich?' he said. 'The mediaeval port that was washed away? A few bits of that are left.'

'I don't think it was Dunwich. It was near a place called Seawick End.'

'Oh, Seawick. Yes.'

Alan paused and we listened to each other's breathing for a moment. I think we had both realized how strange this was: that the day after the funeral of his wife, my sister, we should be talking about an insignificant little ruin on the edge of the North Sea. But that's what happened. On the other hand, if we hadn't talked about that, or something equally irrelevant, we would have stopped talking altogether. I think we both realized that, too.

I also think that, for both of us, it was a relief, a welcome diversion. For me, it was something else as well.

'Seawick was much smaller than Dunwich,' he said. 'No charter or anything like that. Not much more than a large fishing village that coped with the trade Dunwich didn't want to handle.'

There was a rhythm to Alan's voice now, a sense of

purpose. He wasn't just a history buff. He was also a teacher. He couldn't resist an opportunity to instruct someone, whatever the subject. When I had first known him, it had irritated the hell out of me and led to my making bad jokes that made most of the family uncomfortable and Mary glow with rage.

'It's not even on the map now,' he was saying. 'The estuary was silting up by the fourteenth century when the currents changed. Then the town began to go when the sea advanced. There wasn't much left by the end of the sixteenth century. Seawick End was outside the walls and there are still a few cottages there with some very old masonry and some quite interesting windows. But no one really knows how old they are – that's the trouble with vernacular buildings. Even the windows can't be taken as a guide – they probably would have salvaged stone frames from the old town and recycled them. We didn't invent recycling.' He chuckled as if he had produced a teacherly witticism just for me and shot off on a tangent. 'I mean, look at St Albans Cathedral. All that Roman brick.'

I ignored the allure of St Albans Cathedral. 'But what about the arches I saw?'

'They're the remains of a leper house outside the town. Part of the chapel, if I remember rightly. Probably the western bays of the nave arcade, but don't quote me on that. The chapel was intact until the nineteenth century – I've seen an engraving of it. It was dedicated to St Lazarus. The patron saint of lepers in the Middle Ages. Not the Lazarus that Christ raised from the dead, of course. The other one – with sores, you remember? Christ heals him.'

I could almost hear the poor guy disintegrating on the other end of the line.

'Alan,' I said, 'are there three arches or two? I can't remember.'

141

'Only two, I think. But I've a feeling there might have been three until quite recently, within living memory. There are photographs . . . there are some . . .'

'When did they go down to two?'

He showed no sign of curiosity about my persistence. 'I'm not sure. Probably the big storm of 1953. Did you know, over three hundred people were killed in the storm, including some in Seawick End? It must have been terrible. Terrible, terrible . . .'

There was another pause.

Alan said, 'It's the silence, isn't it? That's the thing I didn't expect. And one just has to fill it somehow and hope it all gets better. Though it's hard to see how it could.'

Then, at last, he began to cry.

10

Instant gratification. That's the glory of the Internet, and perhaps its curse as well. You don't have to wait.

Still in my suit, I sat at the kitchen table and woke the laptop. It didn't take me long to confirm the essential accuracy of Alan's memory.

Google Images even provided a series of pictures – among them, an eighteenth-century engraving of the ruined leper hospital by the sea, with the remains of other buildings still visible between it and the beach; a late nineteenth-century photograph that showed the ruin standing alone on the clifftop, with the cottage at the end of the line of three arches; and at least half a dozen colour photographs of the two arches as I had seen them only a few hours earlier, most of them with the fence in place. The Victorian photograph included a pair of tourists inspecting the ruins, while a woman in a long apron watched them from the doorway of the cottage.

I knew leprosy was an infectious disease, which left disfiguring sores on the skin and, in the past, had aroused an almost superstitious dread in people. From somewhere in my memory I dredged up a picture of a woebegone man in rags, ringing a handbell and calling out 'Unclean!' to warn people of his approach.

A bell?

I had heard a bell last night. So had Sophia.

The engraving of the leper hospital showed a little bell cote among the lost buildings beyond the chapel.

Everyone knew the legend about Dunwich a few miles down the coast, about the church bells that still rang on stormy nights, swinging to and fro in the drowned steeples under the sea. There had been a leper house in Dunwich, too, the remains of which were still on dry land. There was an irony here: that leper hospitals, designed to house the unwanted and keep them at a safe distance from healthier members of society, should outlive the very towns they were built to serve.

I typed 'Storm 1953' into the search engine. There were hundreds of results. I clicked on the link from the Meteorological Office and there it was.

On the night of 31 January 1953, Britain had been struck by what the Met Office believed was the 'worst national peacetime disaster' ever to hit the country. The storms were caused by a combination of high spring tides and northerly gales. In some areas, waves nearly twenty feet high surged inland. In England, 307 people were killed, mainly in East Anglia, 30,000 people were evacuated and 24,000 properties were badly damaged.

Almost certainly that was when the cottage and the third arch had gone. But had Sophia and Max been among the dead?

What I needed was this: to find out whether Sophia was – or rather had been – real. Whether she had ever existed. And, most of all, whether or not I was mad.

My mobile rang, the sound cutting like a saw into the silence of the house. I closed the laptop and picked up the phone.

'At last. Where the hell have you been?'

It was Beth. She had emailed, she said, left messages on both my mobile and landline, and emailed again. What did I think I was playing at?

'I had a breakdown on the way back from the funeral,' I said, wondering whether the word could be more properly applied to me rather than the car. 'Just a puncture, but it was in the middle of nowhere and I couldn't find a landline. There was no mobile coverage.'

I gave her a carefully edited version of what had happened and then listened to a detailed and, I have to say, accurate analysis of my selfishness and incompetence. I asked about her work and she asked about the funeral.

After a while she said, 'They want me to stay here for longer.'

'How much longer?'

'Another two months. Initially.'

'Do you want to do it?'

'In one way, yes – it would almost certainly mean promotion in the New Year. But what about us? That's the real question.'

'We'd manage.' I made an effort. 'I know this is important to you.'

'So are you. Idiot. But we can't go on like this, can we? We're neither one thing nor the other. If we're going to have a future, we've got to work at it, haven't we? Both of us. Otherwise we might as well call it a day.'

I didn't reply.

'I've an idea,' Beth said. 'If I stay on, why don't you come over and join me? You love New York.'

'Let me think about it,' I said. 'Maybe.'

'Idiot,' she said again, and broke the connection.

I'm not proud of it. I was torn between two women – my wife, who was as real as could be, despite being three thousand miles away, and Sophia, who didn't exist. It doesn't say much for my decency or my intelligence.

What complicated the issue far beyond love, lust or fear was the simple fact that Sophia wasn't – couldn't be – real. I couldn't smell her on my skin any more. There was nothing to show she had ever existed.

So this wasn't just about Beth and Sophia. That's what I tell myself. It was about whether I had gone mad.

It was dark now. I had a shower. I put on fresh clothes. I cooked a meal and opened a bottle of wine. After three glasses I phoned Alan again. I let the phone ring for a long time. Finally he picked up.

'Yes?' It didn't sound like Alan's voice, but like that of a stranger with a bad cold.

'It's me. I know this must seem a bit strange, but can I ask you something?'

'I'm very busy.'

I ignored that. 'Suppose I wanted to find out more about Seawick and the Great Storm. How would I do it?'

'Why would you want to?' He sounded aggrieved. 'You're not interested in history.'

'I don't know. I just do. Sorry – how are you? And Matthew and Alice?'

He brushed aside my belated attempt to behave like a human being. 'There must be a local history society. They'll put you on the track. Try the library. Or look at the back file of the local paper. That would tell you what it was like at the time.'

'I'm sorry,' I said. 'Mary's death seems to have made everything strange. I wish things had been different.'

Alan said nothing.

'Anyway, I'm sorry,' I said again. 'I hope—'

'So am I!' he shouted. 'Sorry.'

'Listen. I heard something at the funeral. Something

146

that suggested Mary found a way to . . . to hurry things up. Is that true?'

'Of course not.' He cleared his throat. 'She may – just possibly – have taken a little more than she should. But if she did, it was an accident. The morphine confused her. Perhaps it was for the best . . .' He paused and the teacher in him came to his rescue. 'You've tried googling Seawick and the Great Storm, I take it?'

It took me all of two minutes to power up the laptop and search for 'Seawick Storm 1953'. I wondered why it hadn't occurred to me earlier to do something so blindingly obvious. On the second page, there was an Amazon link. I clicked on it and found myself looking at an entry for a title in the Kindle store: *Seawick Past and Present* by Giles Morton.

The surname brought me up short. The hairs lifted on the back of my forearm. It couldn't be a coincidence. Ten to one, Giles was the husband of Christina and the father of Jane, the man whose raincoat I had worn. Either that or a brother or father or something.

The book's cover image was based on the nineteenth-century photograph I had already seen. It showed the three arches of the leper hospital's chapel, with the cottage tacked on the end nearer the cliff. In another moment I had bought the e-book for less than the price of a cup of coffee and downloaded it to the laptop. It was a reissue of a little history Morton had published at his own expense in 1989. He mentioned in the foreword that he lived in the nearest house to the ruins of the Seawick leper hospital.

I flicked to the end of the book. It had all the hallmarks of a retirement project – rambling, overlong and frequently speculative. The last section was called 'The Great Storm and Afterwards'. This part of the coast had been severely battered. The wind had joined forces with a viciously powerful incoming tide. The water had poured up the creek where Seawick End was, rising to the roofs of the houses and drowning four people. I wondered if one of them had been Max's mistress.

The waves had also savaged the cliffs nearby, scooping out their bases until they collapsed into the sea. The wind tore down trees and stripped off roofs. Morton wrote that he had even feared for the safety of his own house, despite its being in a sheltered place on higher ground a quarter of a mile away from the sea, but the only damage he suffered was the loss of a diseased oak that had stood near the seaward boundary of his garden.

The leper hospital had not been so fortunate. A section of cliff to the north had disintegrated at some point in the early hours of 1 February, bringing down with it the cottage known locally as the Leper House and the eastern bay of what was left of the former chapel's nave arcade. Fortunately, Morton said, the cottage had been standing empty since the previous autumn, since the death of the last tenant.

This sentence brought me up with a jolt. I went back to the previous chapter with a sort of eager reluctance – I was desperate to discover what had happened to Sophia, yet terrified of what I might find.

There was no mention of her at all. Only of Max.

'Max Wilhelm Kraus, the distinguished German philosopher.'

Giles wrote that he had come across Max in a displaced persons camp after the war. The two men had become friendly and, a few years later, Giles had offered him the cottage so he could write a book in peace. Max was believed to have fallen from the cliff one stormy night in November 1952. He had almost certainly been washed out to sea by the tide and his body had never been recovered. The poor fellow had been looking for a pig that had escaped, Giles wrote. The pig hadn't been found, either.

I went back to Google. Max Wilhelm Kraus had an entry in Wikipedia. There was a photograph of a dark, handsome man in a double-breasted suit. His hair was greased back. He had a flower in his lapel and he was smoking a cigarette in a holder. He had been born in Salzburg in 1910, but the family had moved to Berlin soon afterwards, where his father had worked as a jurist and where Max had studied philosophy.

Max was interested in conceptions of time, it appeared, and, in particular, in alternatives to the standard linear model of time as a straight line moving from past to present, present to future. An influential pre-war essay of his had savaged Kant's theory that time, space and causality were creations of the human mind: tools to help us understand the world rather than objective character-istics of it.

I understood all this, more or less, but the next paragraph soon lost me with its discussion of Max's own theories: of time as a spiral or a compressed ribbon, and of multiple times woven together in an enormous, multidimensional cat's cradle of interconnected times.

During the war a weak heart had kept him out of the army. He worked as a clerk at a government ministry in a department concerned with housing. His mother had been Jewish, however, and as a student he had briefly been a member of the Communist Party. In 1944 the Gestapo caught up with him. His philosophical views were considered dangerously subversive, designed to undermine morale. They put him in Auschwitz, but he survived. Afterwards, he had come to England and lived in East Anglia, where he was writing a book at the time of his death.

Whatever the entry told you about the philosophy of Max Wilhelm Kraus, it told you very little about the man – I remembered the muddle of books and papers on the floor of the cottage. I remembered the whisky, the ashtray covered in cigarette ends and the squalor. I remembered the bruise on Sophia's face.

I also remembered the blue-grey tattoo I glimpsed on her arm, although it was hard to be sure of anything in the lamplight.

Finally, I remembered that only one Nazi concentration camp had tattooed its prisoners, its victims. Auschwitz. Had Sophia been there too? Was that where they had met?

They lived in the Leper House, these two displaced persons, fragments of the human flotsam that flooded over Europe in the aftermath of the Second World War. They had washed up on the coast of Suffolk and lived in a place built for the unwanted.

So Max was 'believed to have drowned' while looking for the absconding pig. Sophia must have told Giles that. No one else could have done.

The wine turned sour in my mouth. The alcohol made my head feel full of cotton wool.

Sophia had told me a different story: that Max had gone to visit his new mistress, the widow in Seawick End. But, if Max had known anything about the pig's escape before he set out from the cottage that night, surely he would have mentioned it to Sophia? Yet she had given me the impression that it was she who had discovered the pig was gone, and only recently, when she went to feed it – which presumably had been after Max's departure.

There was an inconsistency here. There were two possible explanations. Giles Morton's version might not have been the strict truth: perhaps he had wanted to protect the reputations of the dead and the living, much like Alan's version of Mary's death.

The alternative was that Sophia had lied to Giles, and presumably to everyone else, including the police and the coroner. And me.

11

The next morning I stopped for coffee in Woodbridge and bought a bunch of flowers. I also took the precaution of buying an Ordnance Survey map, which showed the leper hospital at Seawick as an insignificant black mark labelled 'ruin' in Gothic script.

With the map, and in the daytime, I had no trouble in finding the turning off the A12. It was just beyond Pig City, its inhabitants now safely confined behind their boundary fence.

Put British Pork on Your Fork, the sign said. *Put British Pork on Your Fork*.

The slogan by the road repeated itself in my head as I drove towards Seawick End. The weather had improved – the wind had dropped during the night and the rain had petered away during the morning.

The Mortons' house was off a lane that ran parallel to the coast. The five-bar gate at the end of the drive had been propped open. A sign on the gate said 'Lower Seawick Lodge'. I drove up to the front of the house. The Volvo was still there, but nearer the front door than it had been before, so presumably it had been mended.

I parked the Honda beside it and went into the porch

where I had stood dripping on the tiles the night before last. There was a stainless-steel dog bowl under the seat, half-full of water. If it had been there the other evening, I was sure I would have seen it – I distinctly remembered the torch beam gliding around the porch, and its beam would have been reflected back by the stainless steel.

I rang the bell, waited, and then rang it again, this time for longer. There was no sign of movement in the hallway on the other side of the stained glass.

Carrying the flowers, I walked around the house via the garages and into the yard at the back, in case they were in an outbuilding, unlikely though it seemed, and hadn't heard the doorbell. But there was no trace of the two women there, either. Mrs Morton had looked too frail to be able to walk very far. Perhaps a neighbour had taken them shopping.

I wandered down the garden – not with a particular purpose in mind, simply because I wanted to see the ruins again. I know it must sound ridiculous, but there seemed just the faintest possibility I had made a mistake – that I had got everything wrong. Perhaps, when I reached the far side of the field, I would see the three arches on the edge of the cliff, with the Leper House attached to them, just as it had been the other night. And perhaps Sophia would be waiting and she would explain everything.

Foolish? Oh yes, I know it was.

There were only two arches on the clifftop. There was also a small dog zigzagging across the field with manic energy.

A woman was standing by the fence that kept people away from the ruins, looking out to sea. She was tall and heavy, and she wore a bright red jacket. Even at this distance, I knew it was Jane. She turned to call the dog to her.

That's when she saw me.

The dog lost the rabbit or whatever else it was chasing.

153

It stopped, raised a hind leg and scratched itself. While it was doing that, it caught sight of me as well and decided to investigate.

'Molly!' Jane bellowed, walking briskly towards us. 'Here!'

Molly careered towards me. Her tail was up like a feather. She barked, not with hostile intent but to make sure that Jane and I were alerted to the exciting news of each other's presence.

'Molly!'

The dog faltered. She came to a stop about ten yards away from me. I crouched and held out my hand. She advanced slowly and sniffed my fingers.

I stood up. Jane and I were now close enough to talk to each other.

'I thought it was you,' she said. 'What do you want?'

'To say thank you for the other evening. How's Mrs Morton?'

'She's in hospital.' Jane's face flickered. It was as if the bony structure supporting it had briefly turned to liquid and then resolidified itself. 'A chest infection. I've been with her all night.' Her voice sounded angry. 'My daughter's with her now.'

'I'm sorry. Is it serious?'

'It's always serious with someone her age,' she snapped. 'And once they put you in hospital anything can happen. She's already confused. They keep calling her Sophia, which doesn't help.'

'Sophia?' My skin crawled. 'But I thought—'

'Yes, I know. She's called herself Christina ever since she came here. But her real name's Sophia, so it's on all the records and the nurses keep using it. They just don't understand how it confuses her. It distresses her.'

Molly lifted her head and barked. Then she was off again, her little legs a blur of motion heading up the field towards another invisible quarry.

Sophia.

I remembered the last words she had said to me: *I don't want to see you again. Ever.*

'Of course, her blindness makes it worse.' Jane was staring away from me, looking down the coast to the celestial dome of the power station in the distance. 'Nothing's familiar. She's lost her moorings. They don't seem to be able to bring down the temperature . . . Half the time she doesn't know where she is, or even when. At one point she was talking as if she were a young woman and Daddy was still alive. It's so sad.'

I said, 'I . . . I brought some flowers.'

'What?' She glanced at them, frowning, apparently registering their existence for the first time.

'As a thank you. I hope your mother's better soon. Please give her my good wishes. Shall I leave them in the porch on my way back?'

'Yes.'

Jane unbent enough to say thank you. I said goodbye and walked back the way I had come.

In my memory I felt Mrs Morton's fingers palpating my face, the tips dancing over the skin. A different way of knowing, I thought, not a different way of seeing. When Sophia had said goodbye, she also said that she would never see me again.

Was that the first time Mrs Morton had touched my face? Had her ears and her fingers told her it was me? Was that why she wanted me to stay the night?

Because otherwise everything would have to be different.

I walked quickly back to the garden with the flowers in the crook of my arm. There hadn't been any point in questioning Jane. Even if I could persuade her to talk to me, she wasn't the one who had the answers. Besides, I didn't want to think about the implications of what had happened. Not now.

I wanted to go home. I wanted Beth to be waiting for me. I wanted everything to be normal. I wanted yesterday to be in the past and tomorrow in the future. I tried not to think of the alternative, a world where everything was forever floating in eternity, forever meaningless.

A shivering fit seized me in the garden. I broke into a run. I followed the route I had taken on that first evening – round the side of the house to the gravel at the front.

A third car was parked by the front door: a VW black Golf, streaked with mud. A sticker in the rear window caught my eye.

Put British Pork on Your Fork.

'No,' I said aloud. 'No!'

I walked quickly to the Honda and opened the driver's door.

'Hello? Can I help you?'

The words were polite, but the tone was guarded, even challenging. They took me by surprise. I dropped the car key. I stooped to pick it up. I straightened.

Mary was staring at me.

My sister. Looking much as she had when I last saw her thirteen years ago. It was not possible. Hair cut shorter, clothes different. But it was Mary. There was no possible doubt. The same high cheekbones, the same dark eyebrows, the same way of looking at you as if she knew something about you that you didn't.

Mary was dead. Mary was dead.

I staggered. I held on to the open door of the car for support.

'Are you OK?'

'Yes,' I said. 'I'm fine. You . . . you must be Mrs Morton's granddaughter. How is she?'

'Not too good, I'm afraid. Very muddled.'

The voice sounded similar to Mary's, but it wasn't hers. 'I've just been talking to Jane,' I said, the words spilling out of my mouth without my conscious volition. 'Your mother? My car broke down the other night, you see, and they let me spend the night.' I waved towards the apartment over the garage. 'She's in the field by the Leper House, by the way. With the dog.'

'The Leper House? Gran was talking about that this morning. Not that she was making much sense. I think she'd had a bad dream or something.'

I remembered that I still had the flowers in the crook of my arm. 'For your grandmother,' I said, holding them out.

The car door was still between us. She came a step closer to take the flowers. Her fringe parted as she moved, exposing a triangle of her forehead above the dark eyebrows.

That's when I saw the squarish indentation, paler than the surrounding skin. It was identical to Mary's scar, the one she would never let me forget that I had caused when I pushed her off the roof of the garden shed. When she goaded me into pushing her.

I was terrified that Jane's daughter would touch me. I dropped the flowers on the gravel. I got in the car, slammed the door and stabbed the button that locked everything.

She stood there, staring at me. She made no move to pick up the flowers.

I started the engine, reversed, pushed the gear into drive and slammed my foot on the accelerator. The car roared and leapt forward in a spray of gravel.

At the gate I glanced in the rear-view mirror as I turned into the lane. The woman was still where I had left her, still watching me.

The woman who both was and wasn't my nasty little sister, Mary.

12

That evening I drank too much wine again. My head hurt and my thoughts rocked to and fro, like little boats on the North Sea, adrift without oars, sails or engines.

Either I had imagined the whole thing and was therefore in urgent need of a psychiatrist. Or the laws of physics – and God knew what else – needed revision.

For what if Max Wilhelm Kraus had been right, what if time were not straight and linear, but more like a crumpled ribbon or a tangle of string? What if, for example, in the right circumstances, you could step from one point in time to another far removed from it just as, in a game of Snakes and Ladders, if you land on a particular square it can throw you back on yourself or push you ahead? And what if time were composed of many strands, like a piece of string, and not just one?

Did I really want to know if Max Wilhelm Kraus had been right?

In theory, it was in my power to find out more about Mrs Morton, including perhaps whether she had been in Auschwitz and then lived in the Leper House with Max Wilhelm Kraus. I doubted, however, whether I could ever find out if she had been responsible for Max's death, as he wandered along the clifftop to or from his lover in Seawick End. Nor would she be likely to tell me whether it had been she who had made love to me on a ruined sofa on the night that Max died.

On the other hand, the date of Jane's birth must be a matter of public record. That would give me the approximate date of her conception. A DNA test could establish whether or not there was a close relationship between us, assuming I could get hold of a sample from her.

How else could I explain the fact that Mrs Morton's granddaughter could have been the identical twin of my dead sister?

'It's never too late,' Mary had told Alan, believing him to be me, whom she hated. 'There's always a next time.'

The words had not been an attempt at reconciliation. They had been a curse. As a child, Mary had brought down the wrath of our parents on my head when she lured me into pushing her off the shed roof. Now she had given me a lover who was both younger than me and nearly half a century older. She had given me a daughter who was old enough to be my mother and a granddaughter who wasn't much younger than I was.

I thought about what it would mean if this were not a hallucination – if I found proof or the next best thing to it in the shape of a DNA match. That we are other people's ghosts?

So was I a ghost to Sophia, just as she was to me?

It was nearly midnight. I splashed cold water on my face. I turned on the laptop and called Beth on Skype.

'You look awful,' she said.

'I feel awful.'

'Why? What have you been doing?'

'I've been thinking,' I said. 'About what you said about staying longer in New York. I think you should.'

She stared at me from the other side of the Atlantic. Seven o'clock in Manhattan. Another time in another world.

'I think I should come over.'

'Great.' Beth's face lit up: not a figure of speech, that was what it really looked like. 'When?'

'As soon as I can. Tomorrow, if I can get a flight.'

'But what about your work?'

'I'll manage,' I said.

'Are you sure? Really sure?'

'Yes.'

'Idiot,' she said. 'Dear idiot.'

THE SCRATCH

1

The first time I saw Jack was when Gerald brought him from the station. We thought it might be easier for Jack that way. We didn't know what to expect, and nor did he. Jack had been seven or eight when Gerald had last seen him. Gerald appeared to have almost no memories of the meeting.

'Jack was just a *boy*,' Gerald said. 'He was trying to make something out of Lego.'

'But you must have some idea what he was like.'

'Clare, I just can't remember. OK?' He hesitated, frowning. 'I think it was some sort of spaceship, though. *Star Wars*? The Lego, I mean.'

The more I questioned him, the less certain Gerald became even of that.

When they arrived, I was standing at the landing window looking down on the top garden and the gate. Most of the house faced the other way, towards the Forest, but from the landing window you could see the lane, with more cottages beyond and the piece of waste ground where we and our neighbours parked our cars. I wasn't exactly waiting for them but I had gone up to our room to change my skirt. We used to make the run to the station so often that I knew, almost instinctively, when they were due. On my way downstairs I paused by the window.

So yes, I suppose that in a way I was waiting. On some level I must have wanted to see Jack before he saw me.

Cannop was with me. He was sprawling on the window-sill, a favourite spot of his in the late afternoon because it caught the sun. He was lying to the left of the big blue ginger jar that stood there. The jar had a domed lid with one of those squat Chinese lions to guard the contents.

He was dozing, as usual – I read somewhere that cats spend most of their lives asleep. But when the car drew up outside, he lifted his head and stared. He liked to monitor our comings and goings.

Gerald was the first out of the car. Then the passenger door opened and Jack got out. He stood there for a moment, looking about him, while Gerald opened the tailgate of the car and took out a large grey backpack.

Jack wasn't what I had expected – you could say in that respect he began as he continued. One of the few things I knew about him was that he had been in the army, and that had made me think he would probably be a beefy young man, perhaps with a closely shaven head and tattoos on his forearms. Instead he was thin, perhaps medium height or a little less, with dark, curly hair. When he turned towards Gerald, the sun caught the rims of the gold-rimmed glasses he wore. The glasses made him look almost scholarly. And fragile. That at least I had been expecting: the fragility. One of the other things I knew was that he hadn't been well.

There was a thump as Cannop jumped from the sill to the floor. I glanced over my shoulder and saw him trickling down the stairs like an articulated shadow. When I turned back to the window, Gerald was opening the gate, standing back so Jack could go first.

Jack was looking up at the house. He seemed to be looking directly at the landing window. I felt foolish and even guilty, which was ridiculous. Why shouldn't I look out of my own window?

I took a step away and followed Cannop down the stairs. I wondered if Jack had seen me and, if so, what he had seen. A glimpse of a white face. A blur behind the glass. Something and nothing.

The heart of the house was the kitchen, which was at the back. When I stood at the sink I looked down the garden, past the strip of tussocky grass we called the lawn, past the fruit trees and the old pigsty, to the irregular line of the stone wall at the end. (Neither the house nor the garden had many straight lines in it.) A copper beech grew there beside the gate into the Forest. In the corner, built into the wall, was the Hovel.

Jack stood at the window looking out at all this while I was making the tea. After the initial flurry of greetings, he hadn't said much beyond yes or no.

'I saw Jenny and Chris at the station,' Gerald said, opening the cupboard door. 'Off to Italy next week.' He was talking more loudly than usual, as he did when he felt awkward. 'They've a house just outside Florence. Didn't your parents have a place there once, Jack? In Italy, I mean.'

He glanced over his shoulder. 'No. Portugal.'

'Lovely when you're there,' Gerald said. 'But it can't be easy to keep it going when you're not. I mean, what if the pipes burst or something?'

I put the teapot on the table. Gerald took out a packet of biscuits left over from Christmas and stared at it. I pushed him out of the way and took out the biscuit tin and a plate of flapjacks.

'And then there's security,' Gerald said. 'Always a problem with second homes.'

'Tea's up,' I said, as no one else seemed to have noticed.

Jack turned. For the first time he looked directly at me. 'What's that, Clare? The shed or whatever it is.'

'We call it the Hovel,' I said. 'Or rather, the children did when they were little and the name stuck.'

'Quaint, isn't it?' Gerald said, drawing out a chair. 'It's a squatter's cottage, probably.'

'Squatters? Here in the country?'

'Oh yes. The Forest was Crown land, you see, and the boundaries have always been fluid. In the old days, they say, people had a right to put up a house on a bit of waste ground as long as they could do it between dawn and dusk.'

'Like putting up a tent?'

'Yes. A tent with a stone chimney. Once you had your chimney you could build the rest at your leisure. It was the chimney that counted.'

'So no one lives there?'

'Not for years and years. It was a complete ruin when we moved here. It's more or less weather-tight now, and we've run a power line to it. Clare was going to use it as a studio, but it's too damp and cold for that.'

'The children and their friends used to camp there,' I said. 'We did have wild thoughts of turning it into a holiday home and letting it out. But we decided not to in the end.'

'No,' Jack said. 'You wouldn't want to have strangers there.'

The cat flap in the back door made its slip-slap sound. Jack glanced in the direction of the noise.

'I didn't know you had a cat.'

'His name's Cannop,' Gerald said, still talking more loudly than usual. 'Thinks he owns the place. Just push him out of the way if he's sitting on your chair. He's used to it.'

Cannop was walking towards me but he stopped when

he caught sight of Jack, who it happened was sitting in the Windsor chair with the frayed velvet cushion that Cannop liked to use himself when he had any choice in the matter.

Jack touched his lips with his tongue. 'I don't like cats much. Sorry.'

Gerald lumbered to his feet. 'I'll put him out for a bit,' he said, as if this was the most natural thing in the world. 'Do him good, eh? Thinks he owns the place.'

He scooped up the cat, who gave a yowl of protest, and pushed him headfirst through the cat flap. Cannop's legs scrabbled for purchase but he was no match for Gerald's superior force. When the cat was outside, Gerald locked the cat flap.

'Sorry,' Jack said again. 'It's just one of those things. I've never liked them.'

'That's OK,' I said, feeling that, in some obscure way, I had failed in my duty as a host. 'We'll keep him out of your way while you're here.'

As I said the words I wondered how easy that would be to achieve. It depended on Cannop. Like most cats, he generally did more or less what he wanted in the long run.

When we had finished the tea, I took Jack upstairs to show him his room. It was over the kitchen, long and thin, with a sloping ceiling and two windows looking out over the Forest.

'I'm afraid you can only stand up in part of it,' I said. 'It used to be our daughter's when she was small.'

Jack propped his enormous backpack against the bed. 'My cousin,' he said. 'We've never met, have we?'

'I expect you'll meet her one of these days – Annie's at university now.'

'And you and Gerald have a son, too?'

'Tom. He's living in Birmingham, working in a café.'

Jack stooped to peer out of the nearest window. 'How big is it?'

'What?'

'The Forest.'

'Over twenty-five thousand acres, they say, plus all the outlying parts.'

'Can people go there?'

'You can go anywhere you like, more or less. It's publicly owned. Sometimes you can walk for miles without meeting a soul.'

'I'd like that,' Jack said.

He went to bed early that night. To be honest, it was a relief. He hadn't spoken much during supper and Gerald and I had struggled to keep a conversation going.

We cleared up in the kitchen. The floorboards overhead creaked as Jack moved to and fro in his room. Afterwards we went into the sitting room and turned on the television.

'It's going to be hard work if he's like this all the time,' I said.

'It's not his fault.'

'I know. But what's he going to do all day?'

Gerald shrugged. 'I'm sure you'll find something to occupy him.'

'It's easy for you to say,' I said. 'But you'll be at the office five days a week.'

'Look, Clare, we can't just ignore him. He hasn't got anyone else.'

'I know. I'm not saying we should turn him out.'

'I'd have thought you'd quite like the company. You said the other day how empty the house felt now the kids are hardly ever here.'

Gerald had an annoying habit of turning something I had said against me in argument. I said, 'Yes, but it also means I now have more time to concentrate on work.'

We watched the talking heads on the television for a moment or two.

'Nothing wrong with his appetite, anyway,' Gerald said. He stretched out his hand and wrapped it round my forearm. 'He just needs peace and quiet. Regular meals. Not too many people. We can give him all that.'

I patted his hand, accepting the olive branch.

'Did he say anything about what happened? On the way from the station.'

'He didn't say much at all. I did most of the talking.'

'He looks all right.'

'Yes, but he wasn't actually wounded. Not physically. It's post-traumatic stress disorder. Or is it syndrome?'

'What's he going to do with his life now he's out of the army? Does he know?'

'He's considering his options. That's what he said in the car.'

'I know it's selfish, but I just wish . . .' I broke off.

'Wish what?'

I looked at the brightly coloured figures on the screen in front of us. 'I wish he could consider them somewhere else. With someone else.'

2

That was the problem. Jack had no one except us.

Gerald had been his mother's brother. She had married an engineer whose work took him to the Middle East and Central Asia. Jack had either lived with them or boarded at an international school in Geneva. Sue and Gerald were perfectly friendly as siblings go but she was about six years older than he was and they had never been close. She hadn't even come to our wedding.

We exchanged cards and presents on Christmases and birthdays. There were occasional phone calls, though these had dwindled in frequency over the years. Gerald had stayed with them once, quite early on in our marriage, when he had been in Dubai for work. That's when he had met Jack for the first and only time and seen him playing with Lego.

Sue was long dead, killed in a car crash at a busy intersection in Ankara when Jack was away at school. His father had died of cancer last year.

Jack had phoned us out of the blue last week. He had been invalided out of the army, he said, though he was perfectly OK now, really, just a bit jittery sometimes. All he needed was a bit of peace and quiet and time to sort himself out.

So naturally Gerald asked him to stay. Gerald was a decent man. The Forest was full of peace and quiet, or so people think.

On his first morning, Jack slept late. Gerald left for work at about seven thirty, as usual. He was a designer for a company that had a laboratory and offices just outside Monmouth. They made components for electronic instruments. He explained to me precisely what he did on several occasions but I never really understood it.

His departure left me in limbo. Usually at this time of the day I would leave the washing-up and, still in my dressing gown, shuffle into the studio with a cup of coffee and Radio Four. Cannop would often come with me and doze on the sagging, paint-stained sofa.

But I couldn't just abandon Jack to his own devices, not on his first morning. So I got dressed, too, and made myself look respectable. I pottered about downstairs. I had fed Cannop and put him outside before Gerald left. The cat was now sitting on the kitchen windowsill, looking in. I felt irritated on his behalf as well as my own.

The irritation evaporated when Jack came downstairs just before nine. His hair was unbrushed and he hadn't shaved. He looked so young and defenceless that it was hard to be angry with him. I poured him coffee and we sat at the kitchen table.

'How did you sleep?' I asked.

'Off and on. You know how it is.'

'Strange bed? New place?'

'Yeah. That's it.' He glanced over to the window, at Cannop, and looked away. 'I'll go for a run after this,' he said, cradling the coffee mug with his hands. 'Clear my head. What's the best way into the Forest?'

'We've got our own gate. It's just beside the Hovel. Do you want a map?'

'No thanks – I'd rather find my own way. But I can go anywhere, right? I'm not going to be trespassing?'

'No. It's our Forest as much as anyone else's.'

'What about you? I don't want to stop you doing anything.' He looked awkward, as people often do when they mention my occupation. 'Your . . . your art.'

'I'll just carry on,' I said. 'I'll be in the studio – it's at the far end of the house – beyond the sitting room. Come and find me when you get back. Or help yourself if you need anything.'

I went into the studio and became immersed in what I was doing. Every now and then I would surface – once because I glimpsed Jack jogging up the garden path on his way back; and again because Cannop yowled so piteously at the studio window that I had to let him in.

It was nearly lunchtime when I emerged, driven not only by a desire for food but by the niggling sense that I really ought to be a proper hostess for half an hour. Jack was already in the kitchen. He'd found the map of the Forest on the dresser and spread it on the table before him.

He looked up. 'I saw a boar.' His face was transfigured, as though he had just seen the Virgin Mary. 'It just stared at me and then lumbered away. It was like something out of the Middle Ages. Or *Game of Thrones*.'

'We've got a lot of them.' I took out a container of soup I had made at the weekend and poured it into a saucepan. 'Some people say too many. Still, the tourists love them. And some of the locals.'

He said, 'There must be lots of wildlife.'

There was something in his voice that made me glance at him. 'Deer, of course,' I said. 'Foxes, rabbits, grey squirrels, badgers, weasels and rats and God knows what else. And then there are the birds.'

'I guess you never know what you might find, what might be hiding out there.'

'No.' I turned up the heat and began to slice the bread. 'Sometimes you see white stags. There's probably a colony of unicorns somewhere.'

It wasn't much of a joke, but he laughed. That was the first time I had seen him laugh. It made him look younger.

We had the soup, followed by cheese and fruit. Jack ate well; there was never anything wrong with his appetite.

Afterwards, he leaned back in his chair and cleared his throat. 'Clare?' he said. 'I was wondering. You know I didn't sleep brilliantly?'

'Yes. Is there anything we can do to make you more comfortable?'

He shook his head. 'It's me,' he said. 'You know.'

I smiled. 'I don't, actually.'

'After everything, I kind of got uncomfortable about being in houses. Sleeping, I mean.'

I didn't know him well enough to try to cajole a confidence from him. 'So what would you like to do?'

'Would you mind if I slept outside?'

I stared at him. 'But, Jack – you'll freeze. We still get a ground frost sometimes.'

'I've got a good sleeping bag. Anyway, I was wondering if you'd let me sleep in the Hovel.'

'Doesn't that count as a house, too?'

'Not really.' He glanced out of the window, where Cannop was looking in at us. 'It's got a temporary feel to it, hasn't it? Like a shed or a tent. A tent with a stone chimney – that's what Gerald called it. A place for squatters.'

'There's no reason why you shouldn't sleep there. If you're sure you want to.'

'Great.' Jack was almost cheerful. 'I looked in the windows this morning. And there's a sort of loft, too, isn't there, up the stone steps at the side? I'd be fine.'

I didn't say anything. But he read what was in my mind.

'It's not the bedroom you gave me, you know. It's a

great room. It's just me. Besides, it means that the cat can come in the house again, and I won't have to feel guilty about that as well.'

'As well as what?'

He coloured and pushed back his chair. 'Oh, you know.' He began to stack the plates and bowls. 'As well as for putting you out like this.'

The Hovel was a two-storey building with a sagging roof of pantiles. Gerald and I had been full of plans for it when we moved here fifteen years ago. First there was the holiday accommodation idea, and then the studio. Neither of them worked because we lacked the money and the will to convert the Hovel into something habitable, even on a temporary basis, by normal human beings. It was tiny. It didn't have water, let alone a proper lavatory. It managed to be damp all the year round, whatever the weather. Everything we kept there went rusty or mouldy. We'd often talked about putting in a wood burner, but we never had.

So gradually the Hovel became what it was now: a cross between the garden shed and the place where we put things we didn't really want but couldn't bear to throw away. When they were younger, the children used it – first as a playhouse and then, when they were teenagers, for activities they thought we would disapprove of.

After we had cleaned away lunch, Jack and I went to the Hovel together. We kept it locked, because you could never be sure who might wander in from the Forest.

I showed him the ground floor first, a low-ceilinged room with the rusting remains of a cast-iron range in the fireplace. There was a dead blackbird in the grate, a desiccated and dusty collection of feathers and bones. It was gloomy in here because, apart from the open door, the only other light came from a grimy window on the side of the building facing the Forest.

Jack touched the handle of the lawnmower, unused since last autumn. 'I could mow the lawn, if you like.'

'Great,' I said. 'I like gardens but I'm not so keen on gardening.'

'No problem.'

An external flight of steps led up to the room above. I unlocked the door and went in. Jack stopped on the threshold. For a moment I saw it with his eyes: the clumsy stone walls which had lost most of the plaster that had once covered them; the delicate iron fireplace, a refugee from a smarter house; a small window, grey with dust and cobwebs, looking out on to the garden; the beams and rafters rising to the tiled roof that allowed specks of daylight into the room. There was an old mattress against the wall and a cluster of cigarette ends in the fireplace.

'The floor's OK,' I said. 'Gerald put down new boards just after we moved in. We had to take down the ceiling at the same time, but we never got round to replacing it.'

'It's fine as it is.'

'I'm sure we can find you something better than that mattress. There's no loo, I'm afraid.'

Jack shrugged. 'I can go in the Forest or come up to the house.'

'We can give you a potty,' I said. 'I have got rather a nice Victorian one in my studio, with a plant in it.'

'Don't worry,' he said, smiling at me. 'Everything's perfect.'

We spent the next half hour playing house. That's what it felt like – children pretending to set up a home. I even picked some daffodils and put them in a vase on the windowsill of the upper room.

Jack did the real work. He swept the room and brought up an inflatable camping mattress from the house, and then his backpack. I found blankets, torches and candles. He laid out his sleeping bag on the new mattress but he didn't unpack his backpack.

He took off his jersey and rolled up his shirt sleeves as he worked. His arms were tanned, much more so than his face. There was something boyish about his movements – supple, swift, sometimes clumsy.

I opened my mouth to suggest he might like a radio to keep him company. But the words never came out. At that moment Jack was extending his right arm to hang his coat on a nail in the wall by the door. I saw his forearm. There was a scratch on the soft skin.

'What's that?' I said.

'What?'

'Your arm. Underneath.'

He rotated the forearm and we both looked at the scratch. It was about three inches long. At one point it went quite deep and must have drawn a bit of blood. The skin had scabbed over but the wound beneath was rimmed with the reddish-pink of swollen flesh.

'How did you do that?'

'I don't know.' He turned away and patted the pockets of the coat, which he had emptied not five minutes before. 'It's nothing. Probably a nail or something.'

'Have you cleaned it?'

'Yes. It's OK. I've had my jabs.'

It wasn't the words, it was something in his voice. Don't fuss. He was warning me off.

I turned aside and ran a duster over the windowsill, a pointless exercise in a room where the dirt was everywhere. Jack was right to shut me up. I'd been treating him as if he was a child, as if he were Tom or Annie, and I had a right to tell him what to do. But he wasn't, and I didn't.

So in a moment I asked him if he wanted a radio to keep him company. He said no thank you. He had rolled down his shirtsleeves by now and was in the process of putting on his jersey.

It seems so trivial, described baldly like that. But it

wasn't. Two things happened that afternoon which were both important, though I didn't realize their significance until later.

First, there was the scratch and Jack's reaction when I asked him about it. The other thing was that I'd learned that Jack wasn't like the children or even Gerald.

He was Jack. He was different from everyone else.

3

Ten days passed.

It was astonishing how quickly our semi-detached lives became a routine. Gerald went off to work five days a week. I spent my time in the studio with Cannop and the radio for company. Occasionally I would come out to cook or to do a burst of housework. I went shopping. I saw friends. I talked to the children on the phone.

Meanwhile, Jack spent most of his days outside. It was a mild March that year with some wonderfully sunny days which seem to have been misplaced from May. He worked in the garden – first mowing the lawn, and then pruning the fruit trees and the climbing plants and the shrubs. When that was done, he attacked the brambles that had sprouted over the years into a small, vicious thicket in the corner by the Hovel. The soil was difficult to work – it was full of stones and scraps of smelted iron. It took him days to dig out the roots.

Every day, rain or shine, he went for a run in the Forest, and often a walk as well. We saw him, usually, at meal-times, and sometimes he sat with us in the evenings and watched television.

We had the news on one evening and there was an item

about Afghanistan. After half a minute, he stood up abruptly, said goodnight and left the room.

Gerald raised his eyebrows. Most of the time he gave the impression that he noticed very little about other people, but he could be surprisingly perceptive when he wanted to be. We heard the back door slam. Cannop sidled into the room and leapt on to my lap.

'Something hasn't healed,' Gerald said. Then his eyes went back to the television.

The following afternoon, I took Jack a cup of tea. He was digging what had been a vegetable patch, though Gerald and I had long since lost interest in it. It was a nice afternoon and I carried my own mug outside as well. We sat in the sun on the bench under the apple tree.

Cannop had followed me out of the studio. He sat at a safe distance from us underneath the wheelbarrow. He stared at us.

Jack stared back. He seemed not to mind the cat when they were outside, not unless Cannop came too close, in which case Jack would stamp his foot or hiss or even – I'd seen this once from an upstairs window – throw a lump of earth at him. 'It's an odd name,' Jack said. 'Where does it come from?'

'Cannop? It's where we found him. It's a valley in the Forest.'

'He came from the Forest? So he's wild?'

'Probably not, though you never know. He was tiny – two or three weeks old, the vet reckoned. When Annie saw him, he was in the middle of a path making tiny mewing sounds. It was love at first sight. On Annie's side, at least.'

Cannop got up, turned his back on us and sat down again. I tried not to anthropomorphize cats but I was sure that he knew we were talking about him, and he didn't like it.

'We fed him with a bottle in the first few weeks. We didn't think he'd survive. But he did.'

'So if he wasn't wild, how did he get in the Forest?'

'I don't know. Maybe his mother was a runaway. Or maybe he was picked up by a bird or some sort of animal – then dropped. It happens.'

'I bet he was wild,' Jack said. 'Isn't that more likely?'

'Maybe. Cannop's always been a bit stand-offish, like farm cats are.'

'And there are wild cats, aren't there? So he could be one of those.'

'I suppose so.'

'Have you ever seen a wild cat in the Forest?'

He wasn't looking at me. He was looking over the rim of his mug at Cannop, still with his back to us under the wheelbarrow.

'No,' I said. 'I've seen ordinary cats sometimes. Usually in woodland where houses aren't that far away.' I paused. 'Have you?'

'Not seen. Not exactly. But I saw two paw prints yesterday afternoon.'

'I'm not sure I'd recognize a cat's prints from something else's.'

'It was a cat,' he said, his voice rising. 'I'm sure of it. I know what they look like.'

'OK. Where?'

'I don't know exactly. It was somewhere I hadn't been before. The path was going up from the old tram road, and it went round the edge of an old quarry. Quite a small one. It looked as if it hadn't been worked for years.'

That wasn't much help. I knew of several abandoned quarries in the Forest and there were probably many others I didn't know.

'There was a nest,' he went on. 'About halfway up the face of the rock. That's why I stopped.'

That nudged my memory. 'A big one? Very untidy?'

His face brightened. 'That's it.'

'It's a buzzard's, I think. You must have been at Spion Kop.'

The name made him hesitate, but he was too intent on his paw prints to allow himself to be distracted. 'The path was muddy,' he went on, 'and that's where I saw the prints.' He held out the finger and thumb of his left hand, the tips three or four inches apart. 'About that wide.'

'It can't have been a cat then,' I said. 'Too big.'

'But it was a cat.' He sounded like a petulant child. 'I know what a cat looks like.'

You don't argue with children when they are being silly. We sat in silence while we finished our tea. Jack kept his head down. There was a smear of dried mud on his jeans, and he scratched it with his thumbnail. When I went into the house, Cannop emerged from underneath the wheelbarrow and stalked after me without a backward glance.

A day or two later, I went to Spion Kop. It was an impulse decision. I'd been to the supermarket and the road home passed within a mile of it. It was a fine day and it would do me good to stretch my legs.

I left my car in the lay-by at the bottom of the valley and followed the old tramway into the Forest. The path climbed higher and higher. It was one of the paradoxes of the Forest that, for all its rural appearance, it had been an industrial site since before the Romans came. Even now in its green depths you found active stone quarries and tiny coal mines. You stumbled on the traces of long-gone industries: the ruins of blast furnaces whose walls and enclosures looked like lost cities in the South American jungle; the ventilation shafts of the great coal pits of a century ago; railway bridges built of stone where no trains had run for generations; and the wild and impossibly romantic traces of surface iron workings. Nothing stayed the same for long: like any organic entity, the Forest was constantly changing, month by month, year by year.

I saw no one as I followed the tram road – I call it that, though there were no rails or sleepers, only two parallel lines of worn stones rising slowly up the valley between two hills. There were conifer plantations nearby, richly textured like a patchwork blanket made of different tweeds. The mud clung to my feet and splashed the legs of my jeans. It was chilly, but spring was in the air.

Half a mile in, I turned on to a narrow track that curled round the side of a hill. The trees closed around me. This part of the Forest had not been planted and managed systematically, or not recently; perhaps never. There were huge, misshapen yews, oaks and beeches, pines and birch tangled together on a steep hillside littered with fragments of rock. Here was the illusion of a world that belonged to another time, a world where chance ruled and everything was possible.

I had seen no one since I had left the car. For the first ten minutes or so I had heard the grinding and whirring from the stone works at the bottom of the valley. Now even that had dropped away.

The further I walked, the more a sense of relaxation crept over me. I didn't know why the Forest had this effect on me. It calmed and soothed. The solitude had something to do with it, that and the ever-changing stream of greens and browns that dominated its colour palette.

The odd thing was that the Forest didn't affect everyone the same way. Some people – Gerald included – found it an oppressive place. They felt enclosed by it and even, on a primitive level that belonged to dreams and childhood, somehow threatened. There should be a word for this, dendrophobia, the fear of trees; but there wasn't – I'd checked in the dictionary.

Gerald didn't like me going there alone. He thought I might be attacked or, at the very least, manage to lose myself. He was a practical man so he bought me a compass and a rape alarm, which I generally left in the car – not intentionally but because I forgot them. He believed, I think, on some level of himself that he didn't know existed, that the Forest was a place of monsters. He was right. But it was so many other things as well.

It took me a while to find Spion Kop again because I got lost. (That was another thing that Gerald didn't understand, that I actually liked getting lost in the Forest, because I knew that sooner or later I would find my way again.) When at last I reached the quarry, I approached it from a direction I didn't expect. It revealed itself in a theatrical way that made me catch my breath.

Spion Kop was a ragged hole hacked into a slope of local sandstone. Great blocks of stone were scattered around its perimeter, some partly cut, but most of them still as they had been when they were dragged up from the quarry. Trees, saplings and bushes had softened the harshness of the place. They also shrouded and protected it. The buzzard's nest was still there, a large and very untidy cluster of twigs placed in a low semicircular niche about halfway up an almost sheer rockface. Taken all in all, it was a dream landscape, one that had wandered out of the sort of fairytale that had a good chance of ending badly.

The path passed between two blocks of stone, smeared with lichen and partly enveloped by a yew tree. I paused between them, my eye caught by the pattern of the tree roots and the way they curled around the rock, forcing their way into cracks, slowly strangling it; for, in the Forest, the soft conquered the hard.

At that moment I saw a trainer and part of a leg. I drew back, suddenly cautious. I shifted to one side and peered around the corner of the stone.

It was Jack. He was lying on his front and looking into the quarry. In order to reach the edge, he must have struggled through the tangle of rusting barbed wire that was meant to prevent passing members of the public from plunging to their doom. I couldn't see his face but I saw his head rotating slowly from left to right, as if he were making a methodical survey of the quarry floor.

I drew back. My being here at the same time as him was pure coincidence. But he wouldn't know that. He might think I had followed him, that I was stalking him.

I didn't want to disturb him. I retreated as quietly as I had come.

I was on edge. That's one reason why I didn't take much notice of what happened next. Even now I'm not sure if I imagined it.

As I slipped away, I thought I saw something move very quickly on the edge of my range of vision. There was a sense of something sinuous, black and swift-moving. I turned my head but it was too late.

If there had been something, it had gone. I was left with the sense that, just as I had been watching Jack, someone or something had been watching me.

4

'Spion Kop,' Gerald said, 'was one of those thoroughly stupid battles that the British seem to like so much. Like the Charge of the Light Brigade or Dunkirk. Everyone else tries to forget their military disasters. But we commemorate them.'

Gerald looked challengingly at us, as if daring us to disagree. He fancied himself as a bit of a historian, largely because he watched a lot of historical documentaries on TV. I nodded, though my mind was going over tomorrow's work in the studio. Jack sipped his wine. His eyes were restless, and I guess he wanted to slip away to the Hovel as soon as he decently could.

'South Africa?' I said.

'Second Boer War.' Gerald emptied the rest of the wine into our glasses. 'It was embarrassing. A few Boer farmers against the might of the British Empire. Did you know one reason the British moved so slowly was because of all the officers' baggage? The general – what was his name? – brought along a fully equipped kitchen and a cast-iron bathroom.'

Cannop was scratching on the kitchen window, demanding to be let in.

'It's always the same. Take Dunkirk, for example . . .'

I tried to find a way to change the subject without hurting anyone's feelings. But Gerald in the grip of an enthusiasm needed an act of God to stop him.

'You'd think one of the good things about losing the Empire would be that we wouldn't have any more imperialist disasters to celebrate back home . . .'

Here it comes, I thought.

'. . . but no. First there's Iraq, and then Afghanistan.'

Jack put his glass very carefully on the table. He stood up.

'It's the national psyche, if you ask me—' Gerald broke off. 'Are you OK?'

'Yes, fine.' Jack sidled towards the door. 'Just a bit tired. Think I overdid it today. Those brambles are fighting back.'

'Anything I can get you?' I said.

'No thanks.' He smiled in a half-hearted way. 'I just need an early night. Goodnight.'

He opened the back door. Cannop slipped between his legs and went to ground under the table. Jack went outside and closed the door.

'What's wrong with him?' Gerald said. 'A bit rude, wasn't it, going off like that.'

'I think it was you talking about military disasters that upset him.'

'But I was putting a historical perspective on it. I thought he'd find it interesting. As an ex-soldier.'

'I don't think Jack finds Afghanistan interesting. Not exactly.'

'But I was talking generally.'

I wanted to throw something at my husband. 'I know you were. But Jack's just back from Afghanistan. He was given an honourable discharge, or whatever they call it. And something happened there, didn't it? Something that's caused post-traumatic stress.'

'He seems perfectly normal to me most of the time. Bit odd about the cat, I grant you that. But that's all, really.'

'You're not here most of the time. I am.'

'I wonder what it was,' Gerald said.

'What what was?'

'The thing that caused the stress.'

'Better not to know. And for God's sake don't ask him. Promise me.'

We cleared away and went into the sitting room. Gerald wasn't an unkind man and he certainly wasn't stupid. But sometimes he could be slow about catching on.

Gerald had an early start – a meeting with a client in London in the morning – so he went to bed early. I stayed downstairs.

It was a clear night. When I took the food waste out to the bin, I lingered outside to admire the stars for a moment. It's very dark outside where we live, and it took my eyes a moment to adjust.

I glanced down the garden, towards the Hovel. I smelled tobacco. A tiny red glow was coming from the bench.

'Jack?'

'Hi.'

I picked my way through the darkness, navigating by the cigarette. I stopped when I was three yards away from the bench.

'Are you OK?'

'Yeah. Fine.'

'I hope we didn't drive you away. You know – Gerald talking like that.'

The tip glowed more brightly. 'No worries.'

'Mind if I sit?'

'Be my guest.' He shifted along the bench. He held up the cigarette. 'Do you mind?'

'Not at all.' I sat down. 'About Gerald: he didn't mean

anything, you know. He just gets a bit carried away sometimes.'

'Don't we all?'

He sucked on the cigarette and I glimpsed his profile, in the red haze. It was cold on the bench. I felt the damp seeping through my skirt. I shivered.

'You're cold.'

'Just a bit chilly.'

'Here – take this.'

He struggled out of his jacket and placed it with clumsy chivalry over my shoulders. I didn't try to stop him. I thought it might be good for him to feel in control, as if he were the one providing the help rather than receiving it. It's not much fun when you're always the one that has to be helped. I saw that with my mother when she was dying. Being powerless does bad things to the soul.

The jacket was heavy and unfamiliar on my shoulders. It was lined with a fleece that still held a trace of Jack's warmth. It smelled slightly of tobacco.

'I didn't know you smoked,' I said.

He didn't reply at once, time enough for me to think that there was a lot I didn't know about him, and there was no reason why he should tell me anything at all.

'Do you want one?' he said.

'No, I don't—' I broke off. 'Well, yes. Why not?'

'Right-hand pocket.'

'What?'

'The coat.'

I felt for the pocket and took out the cigarettes and lighter. I made sure my hand didn't brush against him. I wondered if Gerald was asleep yet, and what on earth I thought I was doing.

I had trouble lighting the cigarette. There was a faint breeze, enough to blow out the small flame.

'Here. Let me shield it.'

Jack leaned over and cupped his hands over mine, bringing the warmth of his touch to my cold fingers. I sucked on the cigarette. The flame licked its tip. The tobacco caught and I inhaled automatically. The smoke scraped like sandpaper. I coughed. Jack snatched his hands away, and shuffled his body along the bench, further from mine.

'Sorry. I haven't smoked a cigarette since I was about twenty. Out of practice.' I took another drag, more cautiously this time, and managed not to cough. 'That's more like it.'

'Don't be sorry,' he said. 'There's no point.'

The words lay in the darkness between us. In the silence they acquired a deeper, more general meaning.

'No,' I said at last, 'I suppose there isn't.'

He stooped and ground out his own cigarette on the flagstone in front of the bench.

'Being sorry does nothing,' he said. 'You just have to deal with it, right? If you can.'

I took another slow, cautious drag and tapped the cigarette. 'Deal with what?'

'There was a cave. That was the thing. What happened there. It was sort of OK till then.'

Another silence. I sucked the cigarette again. In its glow, Jack's profile trembled briefly in the darkness. Something partial and temporary.

'We were on patrol in the hills.' He spoke in a rush, as if trying to get the words out before he lost his nerve. 'Routine, really. But there was a mine . . . it was at the mouth of a cave. I'd gone inside but the guy behind me stepped on it. Simon. He had kids, you know. He used to show us photos . . .'

Survivor guilt, I thought – I'd read about it. The belief that someone else's death was really meant for you: that your survival was dependent on another's sacrifice. It made a nonsense of the idea that we were solely pro-grammed to prize our survival, or those of our genes, above anything else.

'That was bad,' Jack said. 'I dream of him most nights.'

I took another drag. For a moment he loomed from the darkness. Not his profile, this time. He was looking at me. The light from my cigarette made sparks in the pupils of his eyes.

'Even so, it's OK. Well, it isn't, but you know what I mean. Feeling God-awful about it is something you'd expect. It's perfectly natural.'

He seemed to be waiting for an answer, so I said, 'Yes. But it can't be easy to cope with.'

'Of course it isn't bloody easy.'

'No. Sorry.'

'And stop saying sorry. You've done nothing wrong.'

I didn't know what to say, so I said nothing. We had already established that there was no point in being sorry. But I was. I stubbed out the cigarette and made a mental note to scrub my hands when I went back to the house in case Gerald smelled tobacco on me. My head was buzzing from the nicotine.

'It's the cave that's the point,' Jack said. 'What happened there, what happened afterwards, after Simon died. That's not OK because—'

The slip-slap of the cat flap made him break off. Cannop was going on his evening patrol.

'I must go to bed,' Jack said. 'I've been rabbiting on and keeping you outside all this time.' The bench shifted beneath me as he stood up. 'Sorry.'

5

I didn't see Jack again until the following afternoon. I found him in the kitchen when I went to make a cup of tea. He was rummaging in the food cupboard.

'Hope you don't mind,' he said. 'I was looking for some salt.'

'Of course not. Table salt? Second shelf down on the left. Or sea salt?'

'Table salt.'

I noticed that the kettle was coming to the boil. 'Tea?'

'Yes – thanks.' He hefted the salt in his hand. 'I want to make some salt water.' He hesitated. 'For disinfectant. Is there something I can put it in?'

I gave him a jug. 'Have you got a cut or something?'

'A scratch.'

'Like before?'

'It's the same one, actually.'

'Show me,' I said.

He glanced at me, his eyebrows wrinkling together in a frown, and for an instant I thought he would tell me to mind my own business. But he rolled up the shirtsleeve on his right arm.

I drew in my breath sharply. 'I thought it was healing.'

'It was. It must have got infected or something.'

The scratch was now an angry red stripe on his skin. He touched it with his forefinger. He winced, though he tried to conceal it.

'You should let someone see it,' I said. 'I'll take you to A and E, if you like. Or maybe the practice nurse at our doctors' would—'

'There's no point,' he interrupted. 'I've had all the jabs. There's nothing they can do that I can't do myself.'

'Are you sure? I could just ring our surgery and—'

'No.' His face flushed. 'There's no need. It's a lot of fuss about nothing.'

'OK.' I turned away to rinse the teapot. 'But let me know if you change your mind.'

'Look, I don't mean to be rude. Sorry if I was.'

I said, 'You say sorry an awful lot for someone who says there's no point in being sorry.'

We stared at each other across the table. Then one of us – I don't know which was first – started to laugh.

It must have been soon after I saw the infected scratch that the three of us went to the pub. It's hard to be precise. The days and weeks of Jack's visit blur in the memory. For some reason it coincided with a period when Gerald and I were seeing fewer people than usual. The children – if one could call them that now – rarely came home, and they didn't while Jack was with us. Gerald was working on a big project and putting in extra hours at the office. I was trying to prepare for an exhibition, and it wasn't going well. And then there was Jack himself, who gave the impression that he was more than happy with his own company.

That's one reason why going to the pub is vivid in the memory – because it was the only time we went during Jack's visit. It was Gerald's idea. We decided we would eat there as well, so no one would have to cook supper.

'Do Jack good,' Gerald murmured. 'He needs to get out of himself a bit, don't you think?'

'Maybe he won't want to come.'

'Only one way to find out.'

To my surprise, Jack was enthusiastic. 'One condition, though,' he said. 'My treat. All right?'

'There's no need.'

'Yes there is.'

I smiled at him. 'OK. Thank you. By the way, how's that scratch?'

His left hand covered the place where it was, underneath the shirt. 'It's fine, thanks. Much better.'

We walked down to the village, which was nearly a mile from our cottage and its neighbours. Daylight lingered, though the sky was already pricked with stars. We walked in line along the lane, with Gerald swinging the torch from side to side.

Halfway down, a pair of eyes glowed with reflected torchlight at the foot of the hedgerow.

'What's that?' Jack said, his voice sharper than usual.

'Rabbit, probably,' I said.

'Or a cat,' Gerald said.

'More likely rabbit,' I said.

Imperceptibly we increased our speed. Or rather Jack did, and Gerald and I matched the pace he set. We pounded down the rest of the hill and walked through the village to the pub.

There was a log fire in the saloon bar – it was cold enough for the fire to be more than decorative – and we settled at a table in the corner nearby. Jack fetched the first round of drinks and the menus. He and Gerald wrangled amiably about who would pay and Jack won.

We took our time over the meal and drank more than usual. The outing had a celebratory feel – we'd spent so much time at home or, in Gerald's case, at work, that any break in routine was like an adventure.

Gradually the bar filled with people. The food wasn't brilliant but the place suited me. The landlord had a taste for jazz and played it with the volume low. We had Duke Ellington and Johnny Hodges that evening. There was another bar on the side of the building with a huge TV for sports, as well as fruit machines and a pool table.

We finished eating and were in the pleasantly comatose state that follows a big meal. There was a couple we knew by sight at the next table – we had exchanged greetings earlier but avoided conversation. Since our own conversation had faltered for the time being, we automatically began to eavesdrop on theirs.

'It's like UFOs,' the man was saying. 'Or yetis. You hear all these stories. But there's nothing to them when you start to investigate scientifically. It's always what someone else said they saw. Or there's a perfectly simple explanation.'

'But don't they think yetis are real now?' said his wife. 'Nonsense.'

'But they do. There was a TV programme about it. Don't they think it's probably some sort of bear?'

'Well, yes, maybe. But that doesn't mean the cats are real. Any more than UFOs are.'

'As far as we know. But if there were going to be wild cats in England, the Forest is where they'd be.'

Jack had his back to the couple but I knew he was listening to them by the way he was staring at his empty plate with such fixed attention.

'Coffee?' Gerald said. 'Or perhaps another drink? Another half won't hurt.'

He went up to the bar. The firelight flickered on Jack's downturned face and glinted on his glasses.

'Anyway,' the woman behind him said, 'these aren't

cranks.' She tapped a newspaper between them. 'These are just Forestry workers. It's not as if they were looking for big cats.'

'Come on,' her husband said, 'the match will be starting in ten minutes.'

They went through to the other bar, taking their newspaper with them. Jack slowly relaxed. He glanced at me.

'Did you hear that?'

I nodded.

'I told you – the paw prints I saw at the quarry. Spion Kop. It's not just me, is it?'

'I wouldn't pay much attention to what they were saying. There are always these stories. The Forest is full of them.'

'Paw prints. I saw them. My phone died on me or I would have taken a photo.'

I shrugged.

The skin tightened over his jaw. 'You don't believe me?'

'Of course I do. I believe you saw something. It's just that I think it's unlikely the prints belonged to a big wild cat.'

'What were those people looking at? A newspaper?'

'Yes – the local freebie. It comes out today. The landlord might have a copy.'

Without a word, Jack got up and went over to the bar, where Gerald was putting our drinks on a tray. When they came back together, Jack was carrying a copy of the newspaper.

Gerald glanced at the headline. 'Ah – that old chestnut. Wild cats. They come round every two or three years. I reckon local papers have a sort of carousel of favourite stories they keep recycling. Like the boar. Or council cuts. Or the winner of the beautiful baby competition.'

Jack smoothed out the paper on the table. The headline kept it simple: BIG CATS TERROR. The picture showed a dark shape moving across a patch of open ground fringed with trees. It wasn't a close-up shot. The animal looked about fifty yards away from the photographer, who had probably taken the picture with his phone.

It was impossible to tell how big the animal was, or even what it was. It could have been a cat. Whether it was a big cat or not is another question. For all the evidence to the contrary, it could have been Cannop.

'It's the same picture too,' Gerald was saying. 'It's the one they always use.'

The terror in the headline was apparently the emotion felt by two girls, aged nine and twelve, who had seen a cat-like animal prowling on the fringe of some woodland near their house. 'They've hardly slept since they saw it,' their mother had confided to the reporter. 'The doctor's put them on medication.'

Last week, two Forestry Commission workers had found the remains of a deer near Crabtree Hill. It looked as if it had been clawed and bitten by a large animal. It had been partly eaten. On the day after, a cyclist from Birmingham claimed to have seen a panther-like animal crossing the track in front of him. He wasn't able to take a photo of it but he did find a paw print, or part of one, in a patch of soft mud on the verge of the track, and he had taken a picture of that.

The paw print was reproduced on an inside page, along with the other less interesting parts of the story. Pride of place went to the cyclist's trainer, included to give a sense of scale. You could hardly see the paw print beside it. There was what might have been part of the three-lobed heel pad that cats have, together with three of the four claw pads at the front of the paw.

'That's exactly what I saw at Spion Kop,' Jack said. 'Only mine was clearer. It was about that size too. Maybe three or four inches across. Just like that.'

Gerald's eyes met mine. I had told him about the paw

print Jack thought he had seen. I gave a shake of my head, trying to warn Gerald off.

For once he took the hint. 'I guess we'll never know for sure,' he said. He glanced at his watch. 'Anything on TV tonight? Or we could watch the rugby in the other bar.'

'No – let's don't,' I said. 'Unless you want to, Jack?'

'Whatever you like.'

'I don't want to leave it too late,' Gerald said. 'Another early start tomorrow. Whoever invented breakfast meetings ought to be shot. But I should be home earlier – probably about four.'

So we finished our drinks and walked back. Usually I enjoy the walk – it's long enough to deal with the lethargy of the alcohol; and, once the lights of the village drop away, there's something restful about plodding up a familiar lane in the near-darkness.

Gerald was ahead of us, swinging the torch. He was telling us about the hotel where they were having the breakfast meeting, throwing the words over his shoulder to us – 'It's a foul place; everything's grubby, and it has the worst coffee you ever tasted.'

I felt something brush my right leg, just above the ankle. I glanced down in time to see a flicker of movement, a dark shadow in the darkness, between Jack and me.

Jack stumbled. He plunged forward and landed on his hands and knees in the middle of the lane. He swore. There was a faint rustle in the hedgerow.

Gerald and I were beside him in an instant. But he pushed us away and scrambled up by himself. He was panting as if he had been running.

'You all right?' I said.

'It's the local cider,' Gerald said. 'Don't say I didn't warn you. It's deceptive.'

He ignored us both. 'It tripped me up.'

'What did?' Gerald said.

'The cat. Didn't you see it?'

'What cat?'

'I felt something,' I said. 'Just before you fell. It could have been a cat.'

Gerald panned the beam from side to side, sliding it along the bottom of the hedges.

'Not just a cat,' Jack said. 'It was Cannop.'

The strange thing – or rather one of the strange things – about what happened next was that they seemed not to affect Gerald – only Jack and me, and in different ways.

I noticed it first that same evening. When we got home, Jack said goodnight and went to the Hovel, and Gerald decided that he might as well catch the last of the rugby despite his having to get up early. I made myself some peppermint tea and went into the studio.

I turned on Radio Three and slumped on one end of the sofa. Directly in front of me was a piece I was working on. I had been thinking about the textural differences in pieces of bark collected from the Forest and I had created an abstract painting based on these. At this stage it was almost monochrome and I had been wondering whether to introduce more colour into the work.

I was concentrating on the picture. My left hand was beside me on the seat of the sofa. I felt Cannop's fur against my little finger. I was thinking about the music from the radio in an unfocused way, too. It had slow, unfamiliar rhythms that originated a long way from Europe. They had an almost hypnotic effect. No doubt the alcohol helped, too.

A minute part of my consciousness was still aware of Cannop, aware of his warmth on my skin and aware of the way his fur was both soft and very faintly abrasive at the same time. I glanced at him.

But Cannop wasn't there.

I was alone on the sofa, alone in the studio. I sat up with a jerk. The studio door was closed. So was the window. I remembered putting Cannop outside before we went to the pub. I remembered locking the cat flap in the kitchen door. I was sure that he hadn't come into the house when we had returned. Since Jack had come to stay I had become much more aware than usual of Cannop's presence or absence.

But I had felt his familiar fur beside me on the sofa. I knew that as well as I knew my own name.

And I also knew it was impossible that he had been in the room.

6

Jack came in for breakfast after Gerald had gone to work. He hadn't slept well, he said, when I made the usual polite enquiries. We talked about other things for a while but then he said, out of the blue, 'The cat got into the Hovel.'

'What? Cannop did?'

'I saw him. He was there when I got in yesterday evening. I opened the door and he sort of sneaked out.'

'But how did he get inside in the first place?'

'I don't know. I spent half the night looking, and trying to figure it out. But I can't.'

'Perhaps he slipped in when you went out?'

Jack shook his head. 'I'm really careful. I *know* he can't get in.'

The certainty in his voice told me something. I tried to make a joke of it: 'You've cat-proofed the Hovel, have you?'

'Yes,' he said, without the hint of a smile. 'He couldn't get in. But he did.'

'I wouldn't worry too much. You were probably distracted by something else when you came out to go to the pub. Just for a second. That's all it would take.'

'But he was in the lane,' Jack said. 'Don't you see? That

200

means he couldn't have got inside when I was going out. He must have gone straight in there after he tripped me up.'

'We don't know it was Cannop that tripped you up. We didn't actually see him, did we?'

'It was him. I know it was.'

'Never mind. I tell you what, we'll have a good look round the Hovel and see if there's any way he could get in. Just in case. Two pairs of eyes are better than one.'

'OK. Now?'

I shook my head. 'It'll have to be after lunch. I've got to go into town this morning to talk to someone who is redesigning my website. And then I'm seeing the accountant, and I'm not looking forward to it.'

Jack smiled at me. 'Sorry. I'm being a pain.'

'It's no trouble,' I said, which was untrue.

'I'll have to find a way to make up for it.'

He was still smiling, but something in his expression had changed. My face felt unnaturally stiff, as if the muscles had frozen with the effort of not moving in the wrong way. Suddenly the wretched cat was unimportant. It didn't matter whether Cannop had sneaked into the Hovel or whether I had felt his fur against my finger. There was only one thing that mattered. The awkward fact that I didn't want to stop looking at Jack.

'Yes,' I said. 'Well, anyway, I'd better get on. See you at lunchtime.'

It took an effort of will to leave the room. I went up to the bathroom and bolted the door. I stared at my reflection in the mirror over the basin.

'No,' I whispered to myself. 'This can't be happening.'

I didn't go home for lunch. I bought a tuna sandwich and a bottle of water. I sat in the car under a grey sky and stared at the other cars in the car park. I watched tired women carrying shopping and old men smoking cigarettes. I watched mothers with pushchairs, and kids trying to impress each other. I watched young men in suits and young women with firm flesh and unlined skin.

I watched people Jack's age.

All this time, I tried not to think about him. But of course I did. He was Gerald's nephew. I didn't know how old he was and I was afraid to ask. I guessed he was at least fifteen or even twenty years younger than I was. Possibly more. I was happily married and I had grown-up children. I was not, and never had been, the sort of woman who had affairs.

For God's sake, Jack was nothing to write home about. He was barely more than a boy. He was emotionally unstable, or at least vulnerable, which meant there was all the more reason for me to behave like a responsible adult. I didn't love him. I wasn't sure I even liked him. But for some reason I couldn't stop thinking about him.

Absolutely nothing had happened. Or rather, whatever had happened this morning in the kitchen, such as it was, had been confined to my own head. And – to be perfectly honest – body. That was the way it would stay. It occurred to me – and at this point I felt unaccountably depressed – that there was no reason why he should feel anything in return. This was all about me. Besides – and at this point my depression grew even worse as I returned to the age gap between us – I was old enough to be his mother.

I talked myself round and round in circles. I had to do something. I couldn't stay in the car park for ever. I couldn't go home, either, so I went for a walk in the Forest.

Usually, this was a calming thing to do, but not this time. I must have walked five or six miles, following paths I had never followed before wherever I could, but never quite losing myself. At first I walked slowly, but my pace gradually accelerated until I was walking as fast as I could without breaking into a run. In this time I saw one or two walkers, and a solitary cyclist. I startled half a dozen fallow deer, which bounced into the undergrowth as if their legs were on springs.

I couldn't throw off the sense that I was never, ever alone. They say we know when we are being watched, that this is a half-buried characteristic from our primitive past as a species. Whoever, or whatever, was watching me was not doing it in a particularly menacing way – I didn't know how I knew this, but I did – but with a steady, unflinching attention.

I set traps for whatever it was, assuming it existed. I doubled back without warning. I glanced from side to side. Occasionally I thought I might have glimpsed a dark shadow, close to the ground, flickering among the trees. Perhaps my conscience was pursuing me. Or Nemesis. But I hadn't done anything wrong.

I waited until after four o'clock before going home. Gerald was coming home early today. I yearned for him, for his safe, dependable presence. He would act as a sort of lightning conductor, diverting this destructive impulse into a neutral place where it could be made harmless.

When I reached the house, however, Gerald's car wasn't parked outside. I delved in my bag for my phone. There was a text from him that had arrived while I was walking in the Forest.

Sorry. Meeting with Brian at 5. Back 7ish? xx

I started the engine again. But it was too late. Jack had come through the gate from the top garden. He was smiling at me. I turned off the engine and lowered the window.

'Where've you been?' he said. 'I was expecting you at lunchtime.'

'I got held up.' I wondered if he had noticed my turning on the engine again and then turning it off. 'I should have phoned.'

'Doesn't matter.' He was fizzing and crackling like a

firework. His hair was even more of a mess than usual. I wanted to touch it, to find out what it felt like.

I said, 'Did you find something to eat?'

'Oh yes.' He waved his hand as if brushing away the very idea of food. 'Clare, I saw it. The wild cat. I took a photo.'

'Oh. Where?'

'At Spion Kop, of course. It was on the floor of the quarry. It must be living there. It's big, too, really big. I think it's a panther. It's certainly not a domestic runaway.'

He opened the door, so I had to leave the shelter of the car. He took my bag.

'Come on,' he said. 'You just won't believe it.'

I followed him along the path to the front door. Once again I felt the sensation of being watched. I glanced up. Cannop was sitting on the landing windowsill. He was looking down at us.

The photograph was a disappointment. When he came home, Gerald got it up on his laptop. We sat round the kitchen table, looking at it in turn.

'I see what you're getting at.' His finger stabbed at the screen, once, then twice. 'That could be a shoulder. And that could be the hind legs.'

'I saw it,' Jack said. 'I saw it move.'

Gerald nodded. 'Yes. But the trouble is, that tree trunk's in the way, so you can't even be sure the two bits are connected. And then there's that lump of stone, so you can't see the head. Or where the head would be.'

'It's hard to tell the scale,' I said.

Jack spread his arms wide. 'That big. At least.'

'So does that mean it's young? Don't they grow larger than that? If it *is* a panther.'

'Not necessarily.' He ran his fingers through his hair, which was wiry, like he was, and needed cutting. 'Panthers aren't a separate species. They're usually just one of the bigger cats with the melanistic colour variant that makes their fur black.'

As Jack went on, Gerald and I exchanged glances across the table. Most couples develop a private marital short-hand, a form of communication that doesn't always need words. We were both thinking that Jack was just a boy really, however old his birth certificate said he was. His enthusiasm for the subject and his burning desire to tell us about it reminded me of our son when he was in the grip of a new interest. So did Jack's mild air of condescension while he lectured us. I knew Gerald was thinking the same.

It led me to think how close he and I were, for all our silences and differences, and how much we shared that could never be shared with anyone else. It also made me think how all this didn't really change anything – I still found it heartbreakingly endearing when Jack ran his fingers through his hair and made it stand up in a clump of curly spikes. And I still found it hard to look away from his neck and its junction with his shoulders. God alone knew why. It seemed such a vulnerable place.

'That's all very well,' Gerald said, 'but just because panthers exist, it doesn't mean we have one here. If only you'd had a proper camera with you. One with a decent zoom lens.'

Jack said, 'I know what I saw. A big black cat, at least a metre long.'

'Yes.' Gerald nodded at the screen. 'But I'm afraid this won't convince anyone. Not unless they're a convert already.'

'Could you lend me a camera?'

'Clare's got one.'

Jack turned to me, his face eager and alert. 'Would you let me borrow it?'

'Sure.' To tell the truth, I was reluctant to lend it to anyone, let alone someone who was going to take it on safari with him. 'But you will take care of it? I use it for work.'

'Of course.' He flashed a smile at me.

'And you take care too, won't you?' I said awkwardly. 'Just in case it is a wild cat and it doesn't like humans.'

After supper, Jack went to the Hovel, taking the camera with him. Gerald and I watched TV, side by side on the sofa with Cannop squashed between us. There was a historical documentary on BBC Four. It had unconvincing dramatic reconstructions that were meant to be funny and a presenter with artfully dishevelled hair and a motorbike.

'Why is he so interested?' Gerald said out of the blue.

'Jack? You mean in cats?'

'If he's got a phobia about them, it just doesn't make sense. You'd think he'd try to avoid them. Look what he's like with Cannop.'

'I don't know. Maybe it makes a difference that this one at the quarry is out in the Forest, that it's wild.' My fingertips burrowed into Cannop's fur. 'Unlike this little horror. Anyway, aren't fear and fascination just different sides of the same thing?'

Gerald lowered his voice, quite unnecessarily. 'I don't think it exists.'

I glanced at him. 'He thinks he's seen something.'

'That doesn't mean it's real.' Gerald hesitated. 'I'm wondering if he's more disturbed than he seems. There was nothing remotely cat-like in that photograph. Perhaps he's hallucinating.'

'He had a bad time in Afghanistan. I told you – having his friend blown up beside him.'

'But what's that got to do with cats?'

'I don't know,' I said.

I hadn't told Gerald about Jack's belief that Cannop was somehow finding his way into the Hovel. I wasn't keeping it from him – of course not – but there just hadn't been an opportunity. When I'd come home this afternoon, Jack hadn't mentioned the idea of our examining the Hovel together to see if we could find a way in that Cannop might have used. I decided not to say anything about it now. There was no point in complicating matters. Perhaps Jack had forgotten all about it. If I told Gerald now it would only make him think that Jack was even more unbalanced than he already suspected. Time enough to tell him when and if Jack brought up the subject again.

That was how I reasoned it out to myself. It seemed logical enough at the time. How we tell lies to ourselves.

We went to bed early that night too. Usually, Gerald couldn't tear himself away from a historical documentary – he adored being rude about the presenter and arguing with the experts who are produced to lend a tincture of scholarship to the programme. But not this one. At the time it didn't seem in any way significant, any more than the helpfulness with the chores had done.

We went upstairs. Gerald was the first in bed. I pottered about, putting away clothes, while he was reading. As I went to the window to draw the curtains, I glanced at him.

'You OK? You seem very quiet.'

He raised his eyes from the book. 'I'm fine. Just tired.'

He went on reading. Perhaps I should have probed more. But I didn't, because I wanted to look out of the window, which looked down the garden to the Hovel and the dark mass of the Forest beyond. I wanted to see if there was still a light in the window of the upper room of the Hovel. I put my face close to the glass.

The Hovel was in darkness. But the light from our bedroom window made a faint, radiant wedge on the grass beneath.

A black shadow cut through the wedge moving from the cottage towards the Hovel and the Forest. Cannop was on the prowl. I think it was Cannop.

When I got into bed I didn't read. I said goodnight and turned away, leaving Gerald alone with his book.

I wasn't exactly happy that night. I was anxious, excited and a little afraid. I was heavy with anticipation, though I wasn't sure what I was anticipating or even what I wanted. But all this added up to an emotional cocktail that was curiously like happiness. As I lay in bed, curled away from Gerald, I hugged it to myself like a guilty secret. Except that there was nothing to be guilty about because I had done nothing wrong.

7

Next morning, Gerald went into work early again. I had breakfast with him and made a start in the studio. In the light of day, the excitement I had felt the previous evening seemed unreal. There was no sign of Jack, which wasn't unusual. He had a kettle, water and tea at the Hovel, as well as a variety of high-energy cereal bars. Perhaps he had gone out at the crack of dawn to stake out the quarry with the camera.

For the rest of the morning, I hardly thought of him. That might seem odd. But, being an artist had this in its favour: it had the power to push almost anything else to the margins of the mind.

Jack still hadn't put in an appearance when I broke off for lunch. By this stage I had persuaded myself that I had put yesterday's events behind me; they had been an emotional anomaly, best forgotten.

I made myself a sandwich and took it outside to the bench. It was one of those improbably warm and sunny days you sometimes get in March. In a sheltered spot, you can make yourself believe you are on the edge of summer. I ate slowly, my eyes half-closed against the glare. Part of me relished the solitude. Even Cannop could be an intruder sometimes. He always wanted something, if only for me to feed him or provide a lap for him to doze on or just to give something for him to watch through his heavy-lidded eyes.

I was almost asleep when I heard Jack scream. The sound sliced through me. The plate slid from my lap to the ground, where it shattered on the flagstone in front of the bench. I dropped the remains of my sandwich among the fragments and ran towards the Hovel.

He was standing just outside the door of the upper room of the Hovel, at the head of the flight of stone steps that lead down to the garden path. He was wearing muddy jeans and a torn T-shirt. The door was open. He was staring into the room beyond.

My camera was lying at the foot of the steps. It wasn't in its case.

'Jack,' I called. 'Jack – what is it?'

He gave no sign he had heard me. I ran up the steps. He wasn't even aware of my presence until I laid my hand on his arm. It was the arm with the scratch on it.

He turned his head to me. 'Look,' he said. 'Look – it's got inside and killed something.'

Still holding him, I looked through the doorway at his sleeping bag on the camping mattress. It was almost entirely obliterated by a sea of feathers. They were white, grey, black and even a sort of blue. There were spots of blood, too. The colours were beautiful.

'Clare,' Jack said. 'I just can't stand it.'

He turned towards me. I don't know how it happened. I don't know which of us made the first move. Not that it mattered any more.

The need for comfort, to give it and receive it, is the Trojan horse of the emotions. Once the horse is inside the walls of the city, the walls no longer matter.

*　　*　　*

210

We went into the Hovel, despite the feathers, despite the blood. The old mattress, the stained, lumpy one that had been there for years, was still propped against the wall, waiting for me to arrange for someone to take it to the dump. Jack dragged it to the floor, creating a draught that made the feathers flutter and dance on his sleeping bag. He pulled me on top of him, and we did what had to be done.

The old-fashioned word for it is lust. It was a desperate, harsh emotion that pulled us together and made us tear at each other's clothes. There was an inevitability to it, a sense that I was powerless. As his hands were tugging at my belt, I had time to think, with a sense of horrified wonder, 'But I'm old enough to be his mother.'

After that there wasn't any time for thought. We writhed and heaved on the dirty mattress that smelled of damp and dust. Nothing else existed except the need to do what we were doing. It was, I suppose, a sort of temporary death.

Afterwards we lay still for a moment. The door was still open. I heard birdsong.

Jack pulled on his T-shirt. He gave a cry of pain. I glanced at him. He wasn't wearing his glasses. He was looking at his arm, where the scratch seemed more swollen than before. The wound had opened up. There were spots of blood on the mattress and even on the sleeve of my shirt.

'For God's sake,' I said. 'You've got to do something about that.'

He turned aside, fumbling for his glasses. I scrambled off the mattress and began to pull on my jeans.

'It's infected,' I said. 'Anyone with half an eye can see that. You're being ridiculous – you're just letting it get worse.'

I was furious with him, with his stupidity. Really, of

211

course, I was furious with myself: and it was the worst sort of anger, the sort that has a dark undertone of guilt.

Jack stared up at me. He had his glasses on now, which made him look half-grown and defenceless, like a baby owl. He was only wearing his T-shirt and his naked legs were thin, pale and hairy. The eyes behind the glasses were magnified and moist. He was on the verge of tears.

'Come on,' I said. 'Get dressed. We've got to tidy up.'

He didn't move. 'I've had it since Afghanistan. Since the cave.'

'Had what?' I was buttoning up my shirt with feverish haste and trying to avoid looking at him.

'This,' he said. 'The scratch.'

My jersey was inside out. It fought my attempt to put it on every step of the way.

'When the mine went off,' he said, 'I was inside the cave. It brought down the hillside above. On top of Simon.'

I looked at Jack. Simon his friend. Simon with the wife and kids.

'Look – I'm sorry,' I said. 'I truly am. But could you please get dressed before we talk about this?'

Jack said, 'I was inside the cave. Don't you see? I was trapped. I thought I'd be there for ever. That's why I don't much like sleeping in houses any more. That's why I don't much like trains or planes or even cars, unless I'm driving. That's why I wanted to sleep here.' He waved his hand in a gesture that encompassed the Hovel. 'It's not like a house. It's not enclosed in the same way.' His eyes returned to me. 'And it's all mine.'

'OK, yes. But if you'd get dressed, we could sort out the—'

He waved me away like a fly. 'But I wasn't alone in the cave.'

'So the rest of the patrol was there?'

'No. Not them. But something was – I could hear it

moving. And there was a smell, like rotting meat. It was pitch-black, but I knew it was coming towards me – there was a lot of debris there and I could hear the stones shifting under its weight.'

It? I thought. *Something?*

'I had a cigarette lighter . . . so then I saw it. Just for a moment. It was a cat, a huge cat.'

'What sort of cat?'

'I couldn't see it properly. Only its shadow, and the size of it. And the eyes. That was the worst thing, the eyes. They reflected the flame.'

I crouched beside him on the mattress and took his hand. The skin was cold and clammy, despite the exercise we had had. He didn't just need a doctor for the scratch on his arm. He needed a psychiatrist to help him deal with whatever was going on in his head.

'Listen to me,' I said. 'It's all over. You're safe now.' I heard my voice and remembered myself saying the same words when one of the children woke from a nightmare. 'It wasn't real. You're with me.'

'It was as real as you,' Jack said. 'So I shot it.'

I rocked back on my heels. 'What?'

'What else could I do? It was going to attack me. I couldn't hear properly for days afterwards.'

'Was it dead? What was it like?'

'I don't know. I must have fainted – hit my head or something. The other guys got me out. I wasn't aware of anything until I woke up on the way back to base.' He touched his forearm delicately. 'That's when I found I'd got this. Everyone said how lucky I was. Just a scratch. That's what they said. Just a scratch.'

'What about the cat or whatever it was?'

Jack shrugged. 'No trace of it. There was some blood on the floor of the cave, apparently. Not much.'

Of course there wouldn't be any sign of a cat. It was

pretty obvious what must have happened: Jack had probably acquired the scratch when the mine went up, and it had become infected, perhaps with something resistant to antibiotics. The blood would have been Jack's, or possibly the unfortunate Simon's.

'I don't know how big the cat was,' he said, as if answering the question. 'I couldn't tell how far away from me it was. And I only glimpsed it for a second.' He glanced at me. 'There used to be Afghan tigers – I looked them up – but they've been extinct for nearly a hundred years.'

While he was speaking, I stood up and finished dressing. 'Come on,' I said when he had finished. 'Get dressed. We've got to clear up in here.'

I looked away when he pulled on his jeans. I was suddenly and absurdly overcome by a need to preserve the proprieties, to protect his modesty and mine. I kept my mind on the practicalities, on the need to get a dustpan and brush, and perhaps some water and a scrubbing brush for the blood. The dead bird had been a magpie, to judge by the feathers. This must have been Cannop's work. He had plucked and eaten it in his usual methodical way.

A movement caught my eye, and I swung round to the door, which in our haste we had left ajar.

Cannop sauntered into the room. Jack backed away from him.

The cat wasn't alone. Behind him, holding my camera in front of him in both hands, came Gerald.

8

It didn't occur to me to ask the obvious question until later. I was too busy putting on an elaborate pretence that everything was normal, a performance designed primarily with Gerald in mind but also, to some extent, for myself.

I kept as close to the truth as possible. Jack had come back from the Forest, opened the door of the Hovel and let out a yell that had brought me running. That wretched cat of ours – which had now slipped away from the scene of the crime – had excelled himself. Jack and I had just been talking about how to deal with the mess.

Gerald listened, nodding in a way that I hoped was sympathetic. He was still in his work clothes, though he had loosened his tie. When I'd finished, he held up the camera.

'What happened here then?'

'That was me,' Jack said. 'I'm so sorry – I had it in my hand when I was coming up the steps – I just dropped it when I saw all this.'

'Never mind,' I said, which wasn't very helpful.

'It must be damaged. I'll buy you another one.'

But I didn't want another one. I wanted that one. Gerald had given it to me for my last birthday.

'I hope the memory card's OK,' he went on.

So did I: there were four months' worth of photographs on there, including my visual working notes for the next exhibition.

Jack looked from Gerald to me. 'I got a really good shot of it.'

'Of what?' Gerald said.

'The wild cat at Spion Kop. It's huge. You just won't believe it.'

'I'm going to clear up,' I said, suddenly sick of hearing about Jack's phantom cat, and ashamed of myself for what I had done.

We sorted out the mess in the Hovel. Afterwards, the three of us trailed up the garden to the house. Gerald went upstairs and changed out of his work clothes. While I made tea, Jack ejected the card from the camera. Then he paced up and down the kitchen while Cannop inspected us from the windowsill. Jack and I didn't talk to one another while we were alone. We avoided meeting each other's eyes.

When Gerald returned he had his laptop under his arm. We sat at the table. It was an elderly computer and it took a while to fire up.

Jack rubbed invisible spots on the pine tabletop. A muscle twitched in his face. The silence between us went on too long.

'You're back early,' I said to Gerald, trying to lighten the tone. 'Given you a holiday, have they?'

'There's some work I can do at home,' he said. 'I can concentrate better without those phones ringing all the time. Or people stopping by for a chat.' He looked away from me. 'Sometimes I'd give anything for a bit of peace and quiet.'

I wondered if that was a dig at Jack.

The laptop's screen came alive.

'Let's have that card then.'

Gerald held out his hand. Jack hesitated and then gave him the flashcard almost with reluctance. Gerald pushed it into the machine. The two men stared at the screen, waiting for it to register the card's presence.

Nothing happened.

'Why isn't it showing up?' Jack said, an edge of panic to his voice.

'It's damaged,' Gerald said. 'That's obvious.'

'But it can't be,' I said. 'All my stuff's on it. There must be something you can do.'

He shook his head. 'I doubt it. I can try, but I wouldn't get your hopes up. Nothing was backed up?'

'No.'

He glanced away from me, at the laptop. But he couldn't quite hide the expression on his face: the hint of triumph. He had been advising me to do regular backups for months, if not years, but I had never seemed to get round to it.

'But what about my pictures?' Jack said. 'The ones I took today.'

'You've lost them,' Gerald said. He didn't even try to sound sympathetic. 'You'd better get used to it, hadn't you?'

For the rest of the day I walked on eggshells, waiting for something to break. Walked? I didn't walk, I tiptoed.

The question I couldn't even begin to think about, let alone ask, was whether Gerald had seen or heard Jack and me before he had appeared in the doorway with my ruined camera in his hand. Gerald was a big man but he moved quietly when he wanted to. Had he heard Jack telling me about the cat and the cave? Had he seen us half dressed? Had he seen us grappling together on that filthy mattress?

Part of me wanted to tell Gerald, to make a clean breast

of it all. I wanted him to understand how helpless I had felt. I wanted him to realize that I didn't choose this to happen, how little I had wanted it.

But I had chosen. In these matters there is always a choice, however much we pretend afterwards that there wasn't.

Also, I wanted to tell Gerald in the hope that he would forgive me, which would make me feel better. On the other hand, I argued with myself, if he didn't already know, then telling him – especially for my own selfish reasons – would hurt him unbearably. So I should simply accept that the consequences of my not telling him were part of the punishment for what I had done.

On the surface, everything was normal that evening. We made supper together; Jack ate with us. Jack apologized for my camera again and asked for our bank details, so he could transfer some money to our account. Gerald said he thought the insurance would cover it.

Gerald and I watched TV for a while afterwards, with Cannop purring quietly on my lap and occasionally digging his claws deep into my leg with the luxurious deliberation of a cat enjoying a well-deserved pleasure. Gerald went upstairs, while I tidied up.

The bedroom was in darkness when I came up, so I slid into bed beside him as gently as possible. I lay there for a moment and listened to his slow, regular breathing. I was relieved he was asleep.

But he wasn't. Without warning, he turned towards me. 'Clare? I'm going to have a word with Jack tomorrow.'

'Oh,' I said. 'What about?' My fists clenched of their own accord.

'He's been here quite a while now,' Gerald said. 'It's time he moved on.'

'Yes. Maybe.' Relief made me overenthusiastic. 'It – it'd be nice to have the place to ourselves again.'

I listened to Gerald breathing. I could feel his breath on my cheek.

'When will you say something?' I said at last.

'Tomorrow evening at supper. There's no great rush.'

'I wonder where he'll go.'

'He's got a flat in London,' Gerald said.

'Has he? I didn't know.'

'It belonged to his parents.' He hesitated. 'I think we've done all we can for him.'

'Oh yes,' I said, too quickly.

'And more. Besides, he's got to get on with life sooner or later.' He fell silent for a moment and I listened to his breathing. Then: 'He needs help that we can't give him. He's more than odd. Spending all his time in the Hovel or in the Forest. And this thing about the cat. It's not normal.'

'No,' I said.

The mattress rocked as Gerald leaned over to peck my cheek. 'Goodnight.'

'Goodnight,' I said.

I lay there listening to his breathing until a faint grey line appeared between the curtains.

9

Jack came in for breakfast the following morning before Gerald had left.

'What are you doing today?' Gerald asked him, and his casual tone sounded false to my ears.

'I'll go to Spion Kop again, I think. I'll see if I can get a better picture on my phone.'

He was rubbing his arm as he spoke. I couldn't help asking him if it was OK.

'It's fine. Just healing.'

'Do you want some disinfectant? A dressing?'

'No, no,' he said, pushing back his chair. 'I'll be off then.'

He said goodbye and left by the back door. The cat came in as he left.

Gerald topped up his coffee. 'What's wrong with his arm?'

'He's got a scratch on it. It looked quite nasty the other day, but he keeps saying it's fine. He's had it for months, and he won't have it seen to properly.'

'At that age, they still think they're indestructible,' Gerald said.

* * *

I thought it must be a good sign that Gerald went off to work at the usual time. Surely he wouldn't have left us so easily if he had known what had happened in the Hovel yesterday? If he had had even the slightest suspicion, there would have been some trace of it in his manner.

Gerald had been gone for less than five minutes when the kitchen door opened. Cannop came in first, tail in the air, followed at a safe distance by Jack.

I must have shown the alarm I felt in my face.

'It's OK,' Jack said. He took off his glasses and rubbed his eyes. 'I just wanted to tell you that I think I'd better go.'

'What? You mean leave?'

He nodded. 'Can't stay here for ever, can I?'

'Has Gerald said something?'

'No, but – you know – after yesterday – maybe it's for the best.' He looked steadily at me, though I knew he couldn't see me properly without his glasses on. 'Don't you agree?'

'Yes,' I said, feeling a mixture of relief and sadness wash over me. 'Maybe it is for the best.'

'Could you take me to the station? Or I could phone for a taxi.'

'Today? That soon?'

'Why not?' he said. 'I haven't got much packing to do. I thought perhaps this afternoon, if it would suit you.'

'But you won't see Gerald if you go then. I'm sure he'd want to say goodbye.'

Jack was still looking at me. 'I'd rather go now. If you don't mind.'

'Of course. We could look up the train times. When would you like to leave?'

'About three?'

I nodded, not trusting myself to speak.

Jack cleared his throat. 'I'm going for a walk. I want

to go back to Spion Kop this morning. It's my last chance of getting a decent picture of the cat, even if it's only on the phone camera.'

He paused. I wondered if he hoped I would offer to come with him. But at that moment Cannop jumped up to my lap and butted his head against my hand, demanding attention. Jack moved nearer the open door. He waited.

In the end I said, 'I'll see you at lunchtime. It'll just be bread and cheese or something.'

'Great,' he said. 'I'll see you around midday probably.'

Cannop was purring now. He and I watched Jack walking down the garden towards the Hovel and the Forest beyond.

His going left a void. I found it hard to concentrate on anything, let alone on work. I wasted almost an hour on vacuuming and dusting. I went into the studio but frittered away the time in tidying up rather than working. I had Radio Three on and, almost before I realized it, I found myself weeping quietly at the sadness of the music.

I had lunch, such as it was, on the kitchen table by twelve thirty. (I had fought the temptation to do it before, in case Jack turned up sooner than expected.) I'd done my hair again, too, and checked my face and changed out of my working clothes. Vanity is a strangely persistent and pointless impulse.

One o'clock passed, and he still hadn't come. I waited until then before I allowed myself to go to the Hovel. I climbed the steps and banged on the door. There was no answer.

I tried again and, after a moment or two, tried the handle. The door was locked.

'Hello?' I said. 'Jack? Are you there?'

I returned to the house. I tried phoning him but there was no answer. Perhaps he couldn't get a signal at Spion

Kop. I made myself eat some lunch, but the food tasted like cardboard. Ten minutes later I went back to the Hovel with the spare key in my hand.

There was no answer to my knock. I called Jack's name. The only sound was birdsong. I unlocked the door and pushed it open.

The room was empty. A dark feather fluttered across the floor, driven by the draught. I tried to avoid looking at the filthy mattress propped against the wall. His backpack was leaning against the solitary chair, with his rolled-up sleeping bag attached to it. The camping mattress had been deflated and stowed away in its bag. To all intents and purposes, he had already left.

The speed of it took my breath away. It wasn't any use telling myself that I had no reason to feel surprised, let alone hurt or deprived in a mysterious way I didn't want to analyse. But I felt all of those things.

In a while I left the Hovel, locking the door behind me. Cannop was waiting for me at the kitchen door, demanding food. After I had fed him I didn't know what to do. An hour crawled by. I wasn't hungry. I made myself tea but left it to go cold. If Jack wasn't back soon he wouldn't have time for lunch before he left. If he was much later, he wouldn't have left before Gerald returned.

I thought about walking to Spion Kop but there was more than one way to get there and I was afraid of missing him. Besides, I couldn't be sure he would be there. I tried phoning him again, but as before my call went straight to voicemail.

At about half past two, I became gradually aware that there was a faint clattering outside. The sound wasn't loud and it fluctuated in volume. I paid no attention at first. Then, suddenly, I was irritated by it.

I went into the garden. The sound was much louder outside. It came from the Forest.

I knew what it was and I could not understand why I had not recognized it sooner. The noise increased and I saw a dark speck tracing an invisible pattern in the grey sky. It was the Police Air Service helicopter. There was no reason to connect it with Jack, I told myself. But all the same I knew beyond all doubt that something had happened to him.

I had to ring the police. I should have done it sooner. First, though, I needed to contact Gerald, just in case Jack had been in touch with him, because the police would want to know that. And also, I reminded myself, because Gerald had a right to know what was happening.

In the house, I dialled his direct line. It wasn't Gerald who answered but the PA he shared with two colleagues. I knew her voice quite well – I had met her often at office parties over the years, and she had been here for lunch once or twice.

'Alex? It's Clare. Is Gerald around?'

There was a silence on the other end of the phone. Then: 'Isn't he with you?'

I felt cold fingers squeezing my heart. 'Of course he isn't. He's at work.'

'But, Clare – hasn't he told you?'

'Told me what?'

'Oh God,' Alex said. 'I'm so sorry. Gerald's not working here any more.'

'What do you mean? He's had to go to Cardiff or something?'

'No,' she said. 'He doesn't work for the company at all. They decided to let him go.'

10

If anyone has compiled a *Dictionary of Hateful Euphemisms*, 'let go' deserves its place of dishonour. It's not a pleasant thing to sack someone, but you make it worse by implying you do it with regret; it's a euphemism designed to salve the conscience of the person who has done the sacking rather than to console the person who has been sacked.

That's what I was thinking when I put down the phone without even saying goodbye to Alex. It was a delaying tactic: a pathetically inadequate way of postponing what I really needed to think about: the fact that my husband hadn't told me that yesterday afternoon, just after lunch, he had been called into his manager's office and sacked.

The company had foreign owners. Their senior executives were wont to descend on the UK headquarters at a moment's notice and make sweeping changes. When they sacked people, Gerald had told me, the victims had to clear their desks under the eyes of their line manager. Then they surrendered their security passes and were escorted from the building, usually within the hour. The contents of Gerald's desk were probably in the boot of his car.

Gerald and I had been married for well over twenty years. I had thought him incapable of surprising me. What made it so extraordinarily bizarre was that he had gone out this morning in the usual way: he had been wearing his second-best suit and the tie I'd made him buy in the Christmas sales; he had taken his briefcase and his packed lunch; he had kissed me on the cheek and said he would see me later. Just as he had done a thousand times before.

My legs were weak, as if I had just left my bed after a few days' illness. I walked into the sitting room and slumped on to the sofa. Cannop jumped on my lap and purred with a callous lack of interest in what I might be feeling.

So that was why Gerald had come home early yesterday, that was why he had come to the Hovel. Had he changed his mind about telling me he had lost his job when he found me there with Jack? When he had seen whatever he had seen and heard whatever he had heard?

I had thought it impossible for me to feel guiltier than I did. But I was wrong. I had not only betrayed Gerald with his own nephew but I had done so on the very day he had been sacked.

This started another train of thought: what would the loss of the job mean to Gerald, to us? He wouldn't find it easy to get another job, not at his age and not around here. There would be a redundancy payment, presumably, but that wouldn't last us long. The mortgage on the house still had twelve years to run. What would we live on? My earnings barely kept me in materials.

But there was another more urgent question – or rather two of them. Where was Gerald now? And what was he doing?

All this time, during the phone call to Alex and afterwards, I had been aware of the distant buzzing of the police helicopter.

I pushed the cat off my lap and went outside. The

226

helicopter was miles away over the Forest. It was no longer making broad sweeps across the sky. It was hovering over a particular spot.

The trouble was, I didn't know where. As far as I could tell it was in the general direction of Spion Kop, which was tucked away beyond several slopes of wooded hills. But that was all I knew. It was hard to estimate how far away the helicopter was. The Forest is a place that defies easy measurement.

I called Jack's mobile again and then Gerald's. In both cases, I went straight to voicemail. Then I did the only thing left: I called the emergency services and asked for the police.

When Gerald came home at last, he wasn't wearing the tie we had bought in the Christmas sale, and his second-best suit was smeared with mud. He was carrying a cardboard box that had once held bottles of Sauvignon Blanc from New Zealand. Poking out of the top was his wireless keyboard, the one he had taken to work a few months earlier because he didn't like the one in his office. His eyelids had pink rims. He had been crying.

I met him in the hall. Neither of us spoke for a moment. We looked at each other. At the top of the stairs, Cannop was sitting on the landing windowsill, staring down on us.

'I can't find Jack,' I said. 'I think something's happened.'

Gerald stared at me.

'There's a police helicopter up there,' I said.

'Oh God,' he said, his voice thick as if he had a heavy cold. 'By the way, they've given me the sack.'

'I know. Alex told me.'

'What? Did she call you?'

'I called her.'

His face crumpled. 'I meant to tell you.'

'Where have you been?' I said. 'For God's sake, what

227

have you been doing? I've been trying to get in touch with you.'

He pushed past me and carried his box up the stairs.

'I'm so sorry,' I called after him. 'About the job, I mean.'

He didn't reply.

11

I can't remember everything that happened in the next few hours. Afterwards, too, the days blurred into one another. Fragments of memory stand out, but they are semi-detached from their chronological context. I see them with particular clarity, as I would pieces of painted china in a heap of ashes.

It was a cyclist who had found Jack. I remember marvelling that someone on a bike had managed to reach Spion Kop at all, because it was almost inaccessible, the few paths nearby littered with fallen trees and abandoned blocks of Pennant sandstone, some the size of a small car. The mud was bad that year, too, because of the long, wet winter.

In the end, they decided that the mud might have been a contributory factor.

Long before this, Gerald explained to the police that he had driven around, then parked in a lay-by and, for some of the time, walked in the Forest, where he had got lost. He told them that he had just been made redundant, and that he had needed a few hours alone to come to terms with it. He had been somewhere in the woods between Viney Hill and Blakeney – an area of the Forest he didn't know well; miles away from both Spion Kop and home. He had switched off his phone because he hadn't wanted to be disturbed.

No, he said, he hadn't seen anyone. And no, he hadn't told his wife he'd been sacked until he got home; he had been screwing up his courage to break the bad news.

I remember the two police officers who came to the house, a man and a woman. The woman had the sweetest smile and kept fiddling with her wedding ring. The man had one of those unfortunate moustaches that look like hairy caterpillars.

The woman asked most of the questions. She was so gentle, so kind – and yet the questions had awkward edges and she returned to them again and again. She and her colleague searched the Hovel and examined the contents of Jack's backpack.

'It's amazing really that he was able to function at all,' the woman said. 'With all those pills they were giving him. Poor guy – it's the wounds you can't see that do the most harm. Did you ever see him take them?'

'Never,' I said. 'Neither of us had any idea.'

Her face gave nothing away. 'We'll discuss it with the doctors.'

She was a kind woman, I think, but a professional. She did what had to be done to the best of her ability.

They questioned Gerald by himself about his relationship with Jack and his movements on the day of his nephew's death. It was Gerald, as next of kin, who identified the body. I remember him coming home afterwards. The police officer with the caterpillar moustache drove him. Gerald's face was grey and puffy, like wet newspaper.

He's had a shock, the officer said – it's often a shock when you see them that way.

I'll make some tea, I said, tea with sugar in it.

Who was it who said we measure out our lives with coffee spoons? T. S. Eliot? In our house, we measured them out with cups of tea.

The police eventually returned Jack's backpack. We put it in the Hovel and locked the door on it. I had cleaned the Hovel beforehand, sweeping and scrubbing obsessively until I made my knuckles bleed by scraping on the floorboards and the walls. When I had finished, the upper room was entirely empty apart from the mattress propped against the wall with Jack's backpack beside it. I had been terrified that the police might have found something about me among Jack's possessions, a diary perhaps, something that might have given them a clue about what had happened on the afternoon before he died. Something about us. But there was nothing there.

'Did you know he had all that medication?' Gerald said when we were taking the backpack to the Hovel. 'All those pills? It turns out most of the packs hadn't been opened.'

'I hadn't the slightest idea.'

'He seemed quite normal most of the time. Apart from the business with the cat, of course. But you never really know what people are like, do you?'

The facts were established at the inquest. Jack had walked to Spion Kop that morning. The quarry, abandoned for nearly a century, was a designated nature reserve, recognized as a key site for wildlife. But the dangers of this lost and chaotic landscape were also recognized, to the extent that the main excavation had been fenced off with barbed wire. But this had been done years ago. Many of the wooden fencing posts had rotted; the wire had rusted; in

231

some places you could simply step over the remains of the fence and go right up to the quarry.

Jack had fallen from the spot where I had seen him a week or so before his death. It had been, I guessed, his observation point. On one side was a slab of rock. On the other was a birch sapling whose branches stretched into the vacancy over the quarry floor.

Gerald gave evidence to the effect that Jack had become interested in stories of wild cats in the Forest; that he believed he had seen one in the quarry; and that he had returned to Spion Kop that day in the hope of taking a photograph of it that would establish its existence beyond reasonable doubt.

Jack's phone was produced. The phone's access to a network had been disabled, presumably by Jack. Perhaps he had turned it off to avoid being disturbed while he was looking for his cat.

The coroner solemnly examined the photos on the phone. There was one that Jack had shown us two days before he died, the one he had been so excited about. The coroner also saw other photographs. I hadn't known Jack had been taking them, apart from the ones in the Forest. Some of them belonged to Jack's unknown life in London, but most of them were of us, of our house, of the Hovel – and at least a dozen shots of Cannop in a variety of poses. It's hard to take a good photo of a black cat, as I knew to my cost, and in most of those pictures Cannop was reduced to a shadow.

Only one photograph had been taken on the day Jack died. It was a shot of the quarry floor, slightly out of focus. There was a shadow in one corner that, if you were looking for it, might just possibly have been a cat; the shadow's size was difficult to estimate. It was, the police thought, very close to the spot where Jack had fallen. Perhaps he had simply leaned over too far and

232

the muddy edge of the quarry had given way beneath his weight.

The police had seen Jack's medical records and talked to his former CO. The coroner heard evidence of his psychiatric history and questioned an expert in post-traumatic stress disorder. According to the reports, Jack had at one point had suicidal tendencies. But there was no evidence that these had persisted since he had come to the Forest. There was no reason to suspect anything sinister about the death, nor anything to suggest that he intended to take his life. Nor was there evidence of anyone else being at the quarry, either, not until the cyclist had turned up.

A quiet tragedy. One of the hidden casualties of war. The death was put down to accident.

I could talk to no one about what had happened, least of all Gerald. I couldn't go to that nice police officer and tell her that I had been having an affair with Jack, and that my husband might have learned of it. I couldn't remind her that Gerald had just lost his job, a fact he had concealed from me for twenty-four hours, that he had known where Jack was going that morning and that he didn't have an alibi for most of the day. They must have known all that and decided that it wasn't relevant.

There was no proof that Gerald had done anything wrong. Besides, I loved him, and he was the father of my children. I couldn't imagine life without him.

Jack hadn't left a will. His estate was unexpectedly large. As well as the house in Portugal, his parents had owned two flats in London. These had come to Jack.

Gerald and I went to see a solicitor, who took us through what we already knew from Gerald's research on the Internet:

'If somebody dies without a will, the estate goes to the next of kin. You say there are no children or siblings, and that the parents and grandparents are dead? In the absence of any evidence of the wishes of the deceased, the estate will usually go to the uncles and aunts, if any are living. If you are the only one who stands in that relationship to the deceased, then it'll all come to you once the tax liability is dealt with. It will take time to work through the courts.'

In other words, Gerald would eventually have everything that had been Jack's.

12

I wasn't well after Jack died. Nothing serious, but I felt drained of energy for much of the time, and my moods varied. My appetite was patchy, too, and I couldn't work.

This dragged on for days, then weeks. I wasn't sleeping properly, which made it worse. Sometimes I dreamed I was in Jack's cave, the one he had told me about the day before he died: when he had been entombed alive, when he had seen the cat's eyes and the shadowy shape of the animal. He had fired at the animal, he said, perhaps killed it. But in my dream I don't remember having a gun. All I remember is the darkness, the claustrophobia, the smell of fear and the eyes of the cat.

I told Gerald I thought I had a virus. I couldn't say what I really thought: that I was grieving for Jack, and in shock about his death. If I'd told Gerald the truth, he would take it as evidence that I had been besotted with his nephew, and now I was mourning him.

Gerald wanted me to go to the doctor. I hadn't been quite myself for a couple of months by that stage. In the end I agreed, as much to humour him as to achieve anything for myself. The National Health Service doesn't provide a cure for grief. Or for guilt.

The doctor was a locum, a young woman I hadn't seen before. She was very thorough – she examined me as well as questioned me.

Afterwards, when we were sitting again, she said, 'Is there any possibility that you might be pregnant?'

That afternoon I did the test. To my horror, it came up positive. The question was, who was the father?

In theory, it could have been either Gerald or Jack. Gerald and I were occasionally casual about birth control – all the more so because I had been fairly sure I was entering the menopause, partly because my periods were patchy and no longer regular. (That was one reason why the idea I might be pregnant hadn't occurred to me until the doctor had pointed it out.)

Leaving that aside, I didn't know what I thought about being pregnant. It had been so long since the last time – twenty-odd years – that my mind could hardly embrace the idea of it. I wasn't sure I could cope with a baby any more. What would the children think? How would we manage?

Worst of all, what would Gerald say when I told him? What would he think?

I waited until bedtime. I tried to do it before but I couldn't manage it. When he came into the bedroom, I was sitting by the window, looking at my dark reflection in the glass.

I turned my head, blinked and said: 'I'm pregnant.'

'What?' He stopped in the doorway. 'What did you say?'

'I'm pregnant.'

Gerald stared at me. 'I don't believe it.'

236

'There's no doubt about it. I've done the test. It was the doctor's idea.'

'Oh Christ.'

'Maybe it's a good thing,' I said. 'In the circumstances. A new beginning – for us, for everything.'

'It's not a good thing.'

He turned and went along the landing. I ran after him.

'Gerald – please. We've got to talk about this.'

He glanced over his shoulder. 'If you say so. But not until I've had a drink. Several drinks.'

I was standing in the doorway of our bedroom. The landing light was on and I saw exactly what happened next. Cannop was sitting on the landing windowsill beside the ginger jar with the Chinese lion on its lid. He had been dozing, I think, but our raised voices, and Gerald bearing down on him, woke him with a start.

The cat panicked.

He leapt from the windowsill and streaked for freedom. He and Gerald coincided at the head of the stairs. Cannop collided with Gerald's legs. The cat yowled. Gerald tripped over him. For an instant, Gerald's body was in mid-air. He fell into the stairwell with a clatter that shook the house. Cannop shot past him and vanished into the kitchen. I heard the slip-slap of the cat flap.

I ran down the stairs. Gerald was at the bottom. His head was wrenched to one side.

I called his name. He lay completely still.

'Are you all right?' I shook him. His eyes were open, staring at me. 'Wake up. Please. Say something.'

I snatched his arm and pushed up the sleeve of the shirt. I laid my fingers on his wrist. I couldn't feel a pulse.

Still crouching beside him, I increased the pressure of my fingers on his arm, as if that might somehow make his heart start beating again. I had pushed up the sleeve to his elbow. It was then that I noticed the scratch.

It was on the underside of Gerald's forearm. It was several inches long. It had scabbed over, but the skin around it was puffy and angry.

13

The Forest is a place of beauty and refuge. But there are horrors among the trees, as anyone who has read a fairy-tale will know.

I don't live there any more. I don't paint any more, either. I've rented a flat in Bristol, not too far from the hospital. The children come and see me sometimes. They are grieving but they have their own lives to live. Our house is on the market. They think I'm selling it because I can't afford to live there any more and because it's associated with their father's death. They are partly right.

Cannop has gone back to the Forest where he came from. I never saw him again after that night, after he ran down the stairs and streaked through the cat flap. *Slip-slap*. I looked for a photograph of him the other day, but I could find none that showed him as he really was. Black cats are hard to photograph.

It will take months, if not years, for Jack's estate to work its way through the procedures that the law requires in cases of intestacy and come to Gerald, or rather to Gerald's estate. Gerald left everything to me, as I had to him.

I've told the solicitor that I don't want anything at all that belonged to Jack. I have given her instructions that his estate is to go to the Soldiers' Charity. I can tell that she thinks I'm being altruistic to the point of absurdity, if not insanity. The children have tried to argue me out of it, which made it harder because the money would have helped them.

But maybe the money wouldn't have helped them. Maybe it would have harmed them.

My decision to give it away had nothing to do with altruism and everything to do with fear, both for myself and my baby. Jack believed that he had disturbed and perhaps killed a cat in that cave in Afghanistan, and that the cat had given him the scratch that wouldn't go away. Did he see that scratch as a token of punishment for his friend Simon's death, Simon with the wife and children? Perhaps he had thought of the scratch as his mark of Cain. Was that why he was so desperate to find the wild cat at Spion Kop? In the hope of somehow making amends, of making the scratch go away?

It's the only explanation of Jack's behaviour that really makes sense to me. Given the premise, strange though it is, and Jack's state of health, the rest follows logically enough. He wasn't acting or thinking normally. The psychiatrist at the inquest had made that quite clear. He was suffering from post-traumatic stress. He wasn't taking his medication. He felt guilty for being alive.

Except it isn't really an explanation at all, and I don't understand the sense it makes. Whatever Jack had started didn't stop with his death. When he died, the scratch passed to Gerald.

Had Cannop scratched Gerald? That was surely more likely than a wild cat in the Forest or some other thing with claws. Had it happened on the day of Jack's death, before Gerald came back to the house?

Coincidence? Or cause and effect?

Was it possible that Cannop was in some way connected

to whatever had been in that cave? I remembered that he had found his way into the Hovel more than once, that he had killed, plucked and eaten the magpie on Jack's sleeping bag. I remembered touching his fur in my studio when he wasn't there.

Why hadn't Gerald mentioned the infected scratch to me? Why had the wound festered, just as Jack's had done? Was Gerald afraid that telling me about the scratch might lead to his revealing too much? Had he killed Jack? Had he done it because of what he had seen us doing in the Hovel? Or simply for his money?

All the questions. Here are three more, the most important.

Were Jack's death and Gerald's enough of an expiation? Now that I have left the Forest, if I do not profit from what Jack has left behind, will that be enough? Will we at last live in peace?

All these questions scare me.

I know the baby is a girl; the scan told me that. I know she is Jack's, too, though I don't know how I know.

Every morning when I wake, I feel my belly. Then I roll up my sleeve and look at the smooth, soft skin on the underside of my forearm. Every morning it is unblemished, and I start the day afresh.

But I still have bad dreams. I dream of the scratch.

The *Ashes of London*

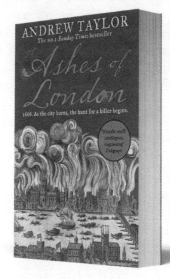

A CITY IN FLAMES

London, 1666. As the Great Fire consumes everything in its path, the body of a man is found in the ruins of St Paul's Cathedral — stabbed in the neck, thumbs tied behind his back.

A WOMAN ON THE RUN

The son of a traitor, James Marwood is forced to hunt the killer through the city's devastated streets. There he encounters a determined young woman who will stop at nothing to secure her freedom.

A KILLER SEEKING REVENGE

When a second murder victim is discovered in the Fleet Ditch, Marwood is drawn into the political and religious intrigue of Westminster — and across the path of a killer with nothing to lose…

THE
AMERICAN
BOY

England 1819: Thomas Shield, a new master at a school just outside London, is tutor to a young American boy and the child's sensitive best friend, Charles Frant. Helplessly drawn to Frant's beautiful, unhappy mother, Thomas becomes entwined in their family's affairs.

When a brutal murder takes place in London's seedy backstreets, it is not certain who either the victim or the killer is. But all clues seem to lead back to the Frant household, and Shield is tangled in a web of lies, money, sex and death that threatens to tear his new life apart.

And what of the strange American boy at the heart of these macabre events — what is the dark secret of young Edgar Allan Poe?